AF256851

Bear Skin
Copyright©2012 Barry Lowe
ISBN 978-1-909934-09-2
Cover art and design by Dawné Dominique

First published by loveyoudivine Alterotica

Published by
Lydian Press 2013
Find us on the World Wide Web at
www.lydianpress.com

# BEAR SKIN

## HOT GAY BEAR EROTICA

### Barry Lowe

Lydian Press

# CONTENTS



** These titles were originally published as individual eBooks by loveyoudivine Alterotica.

† Beauty, Mate was first published in Beautiful Boys: Gay Erotic Stories (Cleis Press).

# INTRODUCTION:

Body hair is making a comeback!

Move over hairless twinks. Stand aside waxed wankers and depilatorized dudes – your bodies look like plucked chickens. Once again, the hirsute look is making inroads into the gay community. Long live beards and moustaches. Here's to the return of pubic hair and furry ass cracks. Let's hear it for thatched tummies, chest pelts, and back hair.

In this bearotica anthology, bears, cubs, otters, and their admirers, rub hairy body parts in a myriad of fashions. There's humor in *Carbon Dating the Bear* when a young twink wants to top his best mate's Daddy Bear; sizzling cuckoldry in *Four on the Bear Floor* when a bear watches his mate triple played on their living-room floor; violence and retribution in a relationship gone stale when a battered partner finds his inner grizzly in *Busting a Gut*; love and hope when an older bear finds his cub in *There's a Bear in There*; and the best kind of revenge when a young twink who is constantly belittled as an ugly hairy duckling discovers he's really a swan in *The Bear's Guide to Depilatory Wax*.

But wait, that's not all, as they say on those home shopping channels: Grabbing a clandestine cigarette on the concrete fire stairs of an apartment building leads to smokin' sex in *Bumming a Fag*; a middle-aged bear helps a gorgeous young twink acquire an extra layer of beauty that only he will see in *Beauty, Mate;*  while a bear meets the wrong master in a match made in hell in *Piss Elegant*; and a bus driver bear is forced out of his comfort zone by a punk musician in *Steam Punk*.

Here's my tribute to those men who have their own layer of thermal fuzz to keep them and their lovers hot and horny on those cold winter nights.

Barry Lowe
Sydney, October 2012

# CARBON DATING THE BEAR

I'm as embarrassed as hell. Normally, I wouldn't even consider appearing in public like this. Naked, except for handkerchief-sized red Speedos strung up between my ass cheeks like those Aussie lifesavers. I hope none of the neighbors is watching as I knock on the door to my best mate Robbie's house, hoping he won't answer the door. I'm praying it's his dad.

You see, I have a problem. I'm 19, pretty good looking, not an ounce of body fat on my slim, okay, skinny frame. Long, black hair, which hangs seductively across my face. My dick is average size, between 6⅝"-7", depending on which porn movie is in the DVD player when you measure. My body is twink hairless except for a clump of pubic seaweed, and my ass is smooth as butter and as bubbly as a balloon.

Okay, what's the problem, you're asking? The problem is I just can't get laid. Let me rephrase that. I can't get laid by the guys I fancy. I suppose two telling points I should mention here: I'm a bit on the, shall we say, less than macho side, nothing flaming, but you'd never mistake me for Russell Crowe. Plus, I'm a top. Sure, I'd love to reciprocate, but just the idea of a cock entering my butt hole sends my body into shutdown and sphincter central locks all entrances to the building.

Oh, did I mention my homme (yes, I'm studying French at college) of choice is a delicious, mature daddy with just a fleck of grey through his temples highlighting his desirability. Hair on his head is not essential. Hair on his chunky body is. The more fuzz that covers his body, the better I like it. The better I like it, the harder my cock gets. Alas, most men of that age either find it too arduous to douche or simply only have time to stick their dick in any available cubhole and squirt before racing home to the wife, husband or spouse of unspecified gender.

I usually satisfy myself with a quick fumble in a borrowed bedroom, a suburban shithouse, or a noirish alleyway, only occasionally going upmarket for a quick blowjob in someone's Ute or family sedan with baby seat attached. Once I encountered a truckie, who was everything I ever dreamed of, until he took off his trousers and revealed he was wearing white stockings and a suspender belt.

No wonder then that last night I was running off at the mouth on meeting a gentleman of such proportion and charm that I was practically drooling. It was the occasion of a charmless party that I'd attended with mates Robbie and Viz. Unusually, none of us scored that night.

"There was no one there over 35." I had moaned dramatically. Robbie and Viz in the back seat were indulging me, though not without a certain amount of eyes heavenward.

"And this was a problem why?" asked Robbie, the perfect straight man, in the theatrical sense and not in the sexual.

I put on my grandest voice. "It's the same problem you will face one day when you realize you are no longer a Robbie and have become plain Rob, Bob or more pretentiously, Robert."

He smiled. "Did that really answer my question?"

"There was a guy in the kitchen said he was 29, but he looked 40," Viz said hopefully.

There was no stopping me. I was playing to the gallery. Actually to Robbie's dad, known to me and Viz as Mr. Wardrop.

"Forty to me is like 12 in twink talk," I said. "You should know that by now."

Viz smirked. "So what is the age of consent for daddy bear lovers?"

I looked over at Mr. Wardrop and tried hard to ascertain his age. "I guess I'll go as low as 45, if ..." Damn! If only I had known Robbie's dad was so hot I may have taken more interest and got strategic info, like his age.

"Cradle snatcher," Robbie yelled.

I had been flirting outrageously with Mr. Wardrop since he turned up in response to our mayday message when we came out of the world's most boring party to find our transport missing. Not stolen, but gone. Our driver, Gene, was notorious for dumping whoever he was with if a stray fuck presented itself. Obviously, it had and regardless of his protestations that he would not, he had stranded us. Problem: Too far out of town for a taxi, too early to get a lift with anyone else, and too close to curfew to take a chance. Solution: Call Robbie's dad.

What a miserable party bunch we must have looked when he turned up. I was so pissed off I yanked the back door open and was clambering inside when his voice made me look up. "Let me guess. You must be Vincent." He half-turned in the driver's seat holding out a strong, masculine hand. His face was tanned and fit, and fucking gorgeous. I wanted to see more of him. So I elbowed Robbie out of the front seat and grabbed it myself.

And that's why I was knocking at his front door. Alas, a very tired and disheveled Robbie answered.

"What are you doing here?" he asked.

"I thought it was a great day for a swim. Got to keep healthy. And your dad has a pool."

"It's ten after seven in the morning and it's 52 degrees outside. The sun's barely up."

"Depends on whose son you're talking about," I said as I adjusted my package in expectation.

It went right over Robbie's head, "And why are you wearing your togs stuck up your ass like that? You better come in, otherwise you'll get arrested."

He led me to the kitchen and put on the coffee.

"What drugs are you on?" he said, appraising my provocative swimwear.

I couldn't help myself. "He's fuckin' gorgeous." I was jumping up and down in my enthusiasm.

"Who is?"

"Your dad!" I screamed.

"Ewwww!" Robbie grimaced. "I wouldn't go there. Anyway, he's not even gay."

Robbie and his elder sister, Kylie, had grown up dad-less after their parents had divorced when Robbie was five. There had been no contact until a few weeks before, when Robbie's mother had announced she was running off with a young shoe salesman and that his dad would be back to help out with his college education in an effort to make up for all those years of invisibility. Robbie wasn't sure he needed a dad cramping his lifestyle, especially now that he was stretching his sexual muscles.

"How do you know?" I was pouting.

"There are no Judy Garland, Barbra Streisand or Bette Midler albums or movies in his collection," Robbie admitted.

"Shit!" Disappointment number one because I am and always will be a show queen. Are you beginning to grasp my problem here?

"What about …."

"No, it's all classical and jazz shit."

"Porn?"

"None that I've found yet."

"That's unnatural for a man his age not to have porn," I said. "Girlfriends?"

"Nup," Robbie replied.

"Boyfriends?"

"Definitely not!"

"Underwear?"

"Boxers. Generic brand."

"Cologne?"

"Stuff I gave him last birthday, practically untouched. You're barking up the wrong geriatric here," Robbie said. "For God's sake, he's got hair on his back. And he never goes to the gym. He can't be gay!"

"Yum. He'll never be able to resist my charms once I get going," I boasted.

"May I point out," Robbie interrupted, "that you are speaking about my dad here, and there is no way you are sticking your dick up his ass. It doesn't bear thinking about."

Robbie pulled a face as I smirked and got instantly hard.

"You're disgusting," he said.

"Who's disgusting?" Mr. Wardrop asked as he came into the kitchen in his terry-toweling dressing gown that came down to just below his waist, revealing his strong hairy thighs. He saw me. "Oh, hello, Vincent. You're up bright and early," he said as he looked directly at my barely concealed erection.

"Just a close friend of ours," Robbie said while his glare warned me to be quiet.

"Is there enough there for three," Mr. Wardrop asked as he nodded at the percolating coffee pot but kept his eyes fixed on the flimsy material covering my cock and balls. "I just can't get started without my morning caffeine fix."

Note to self. Buy coffee beans on the way home.

He poured three cups and went to the fridge.

"Shit! We're out of milk."

I love a man with dirty mouth.

"Rob, be a good boy and duck down to the mall and get some milk and maybe some croissants for breakfast." He took some banknotes from a jar on the breakfast counter.

"Okay, dad. Coming Vince?"

"No. I think I'll stay here and keep your dad company. I'm not really dressed for the mall."

Mr. Wardrop looked me over and nodded. Then he tossed Robbie the car keys and said, "Drive carefully, son."

That assuaged Robbie's temper a little, and he raced upstairs to grab his jeans. Once dressed, he was quickly out the door shouting a departing, "I won't be long."

"Any orange juice while we're waiting," I said as I wrenched the fridge door open. Mr. Wardrop had jumped up to stop me, but was too late. Yes, there was orange juice. On the top shelf. Just behind the milk.

I closed the fridge door slowly and turned toward him. As I pushed him back in his chair, I buried my tongue in his bushy smile. Then I had his robe open and was running my hands through the fur on his chest. His nipples were already hard as I sat on his knee facing him, feeling something else hard, as well.

He held me at bay for a moment. "Vincent, we really shouldn't," he said, but his cock said otherwise.

My response was to grip his throbbing meat in one hand while I fastened my lips to his nipple and sucked. He gasped as I slowly jerked him, and he brushed the hair from my face. He grabbed my wrist to stop me pleasuring him and then engulfed me in his arms. He was strong and masculine. And warm. He just held me and his heartbeat thumped against my chest.

He looked me squarely in the face and asked, "Why are you doing this?"

"Because you're hot!"

He laughed. "I haven't been hot for the past decade or more. I'm not even sure what constitutes hot in this day and age. I do know it's not guys my age with too much weight, a beard, and way too much body fur. I'm so out of touch."

I held his face in my hands and, to reassure him, I leaned in and kissed him while rubbing my hard-on against his belly. His tongue explored my mouth as I sucked, gently teasing him, and then we swapped. I entered him. There was no attempt at supremacy like there is most times with younger guys. No eager rush for release. Here was a man who knew how to take his time. His hard cock poked at my ass crack and I rubbed myself against him. I couldn't help but sigh. Sex with Mr. Wardrop was going to be a gourmet meal not a rushed takeaway.

"Um..." I said as I came up for air.

He sighed. "Yes, Vincent."

"Now that you have your cock wedged in my butt cheeks, I don't think it's proper to call you Mr. Wardrop anymore."

He laughed so loud, I fell off his lap. I got to my knees and engulfed his cock before he realized my intent. I ran my fingers lightly across his hairy balls as my mouth and tongue worked him.

"Ned." He shuddered with pleasure.

I licked his piss slit and was rewarded with his sweet pre-cum. I wanted to taste him bad. I impaled my face on his thick, hard cock until it tickled the back of my throat. He let out the longest sigh I had ever heard. He stood to pump in time to my oral rhythm. It was now or never. As he hurtled toward climax, I gamely moved my hands to his ass and ran my fingers down his hairy crack. I went on. pulling his fleshy cheeks apart, daring to finger his humid butt hole.

I could tell from the short gasps of his breathing that he was close. I prised his sphincter open with one finger. It met no resistance, but as I was about to gently penetrate, I felt his ass muscles grip my finger as he shot a load of cum into my mouth. A few more contractions followed a few more squirts until he backed against the kitchen table a little unsteady on his feet.

"Whoa, boy. With a mouth and a tongue like that you must make a fortune." He grabbed for his robe. "Hold on, I'll get my wallet."

I was struck dumb. I was shattered. Then I was incensed.

"I don't want your fuckin' money," I yelled as I stormed toward the front door almost knocking down Robbie as he entered with milk. He stared at me as I swept indignantly down the front path. Then I heard him call out, "Dad, what's been going on here?"

It took me a few days to calm down, and in the meantime, I refused to answer Robbie's calls or his emails. He was my best friend and I was sure his dad would have painted some crap picture of my perfidy and how I had seduced him. Robbie would never forgive me. Hell, I'd never forgive myself.

It was a different matter when Robbie turned up at my apartment banging loudly on the door screaming, "You blew my dad, you sick fuck!" I had to open the door because my lease specified no loud noise or profanities allowed. Robbie marched in, and I waited for the deserved abuse.

"I knew it was the only way to get you to open up," he said. "Why the fuck aren't you taking my calls?"

"You know why," I muttered miserably.

"So, you blew my dad. Okay, ewwww! Tacky. Bad taste. But you are both adults, so I guess it's really none of my business although you as my stepmother, I can't go there. But you're my best friend."

"He told you then?"

"Of course he did. He was as baffled as I was. Until he told me what he said. So I don't blame you being upset. He thought I'd set it up as some sort of gift to him."

"Gift?"

"Yea, he thought I knew his life story and I was helping him out."

"How?"

"I'll let him explain it to you. He wants you to come over for a pool party and barbecue so he can apologize for the misunderstanding and make it up to you. You up for that?"

I smiled for the first time in days. "I'm up for him any time."

Robbie put his hands over his ears "Don't. I do not want to hear this." He looked at me closely. "You look like shit. I suggest a hot shower, a ginseng scrub and some of that spray cologne you're so fond of."

"How many people are going to be at this barbecue?" I was hoping to get Ned to myself.

"Not sure. Dad was ringing around when I left."

I didn't feel in the mood for a party, swinging or otherwise, but I couldn't miss the opportunity of seeing Ned, especially when he was going to grovel. I skipped the ginseng scrub and was at Ned's place in under half an hour. Robbie told me his dad was out by the pool, although I could hear no gaggle of voices.

I went out through the glass doors and almost creamed my jeans. Ned was lying on his stomach on the pool lounge totally naked. His tanned body rippled with muscle and his short-cropped hair complimented his stubbly chin and cheek growth. His hairy bubble ass pouted like an unappreciated cheerleader at a drunken gay party.

He smiled when he saw me. "Hey, Vince. I'm getting a little burnt. You want to rub lotion on my back?"

"Sure, Mr. Wardrop," I said.

"I thought we were on first name basis."

"I wasn't sure."

"You better take off those good clothes of yours. Wouldn't want to get oil over them."

I didn't want to look eager, so I stripped slowly down to my jockeys and left them on. I glanced back into the house to see Robbie pulling the curtains and making vomiting motions with his fingers.

I mouthed 'Fuck you!' and he disappeared. I turned my attention to Ned. He handed me the bottle of sun tan lotion and I squeezed it directly on to his back. He flinched at the splash of cold oil. Normally, I would have warmed it in my hands first, but I was still miffed.

"I don't blame you for being angry," he said as I began to rub the lotion into his body, the matted hair abrasive to the palms of my hands. As I worked in the oil, I admired his love handles. "I was stupid. Insensitive. I've been out of the loop for so long I naturally thought…" He hesitated. "It never occurred to me that you would be interested in someone as chunky and hairy as me without an ulterior motive."

I massaged his back firmly but gently. "There was an ulterior motive. I wanted to fuck you."

"Yea, Robbie told me. I guess I was having such a good time I didn't notice your finger in my ass until it was gone."

I kneaded his shoulders and neck and felt the muscles tense. He raised his head and half turned to me. "I guess I just couldn't understand that such a young, good looking guy could be interested in an old fella like me."

"You think I'm good looking?" I teased.

"You're fucking gorgeous!" he said and turned over on his back almost knocking me over with his steel hard prick as proof. "Come here." He opened his arms. "And take those things off."

I stripped and my cock was the equal of his in hardness. I lay against his chest and looked into his eyes. "I thought Robbie knew all about me, my life and why I came back into his. I find out you guys didn't even know I was gay," he said. "Robbie's mom and I split amicably when I realized. I fell in love with a wonderful man named Todd. I wanted him so badly that I broke down one night and told Robbie's mom. She carried on a bit but eventually we worked out that Todd and I would move to another state although I would pay support. I was not to come near Robbie as he grew up, but I was always supplied with letters about his progress and photos from special occasions. Truthfully, I didn't miss Robbie all that much because I had Todd. We had fifteen wonderful years together."

"Did you guys split up?" I asked.

"In that inevitable way that comes to all of us," Ned said with a slight ache to his voice. "He died. Killed rather. Hit-and-run. I was devastated. I withdrew. Months passed. Then two years. Friends were always at me to get out. Find a reason to keep going. But in the years with Todd I'd lost just about every one of the gay survival skills. Oh, I tried dating a few times, but always got burned. The rejections sent me into a spiral of despair."

I scrutinized his face intently as he told his story, so intently he looked away in embarrassment.

"Then I got a call from Robbie's mom to say she'd discovered that it ran in the family and she thought I would be a better role model. She bowed out to allow me to get to know the son whose life I'd never shared. It was a lifeline and I grabbed for it. That's why I'm here."

"Some story," I said as I stood up.

"I thought you were a sort of gift from Robbie to help ease me back into the marketplace. Forgive me?"

"Turn over, old man," I commanded. Ned lay back on his stomach, exposing his beautiful ass. I slapped it hard, admiring the red stinging slash across his buttocks. I slapped him again and was delighted as he sucked in air as an expression of his pain. Then I bent down and kissed the warm flesh. I parted his cheeks and kneeled to put my lips to his asshole, my tongue lapping to moisten the hairs around his opening. I sucked and probed as he wriggled beneath the onslaught.

My face awash with my own spit and the sweat from Ned's ass, I came up for air. I was aching for release. I drizzled sun tan lotion between his cheeks and massaged it into his inviting hole. I took my time even though every muscle in my body ached to get to the action. I teased his ass entrance with first one finger then a second. The rhythm was smooth and met little resistance. His asshole was hot and inviting. As I kept up the finger fucking, I greased my cock with the other hand. Then kneeling behind him, I extracted my fingers and lowered my cock.

As I sank into his ass, I groaned. I pulled him up so that we were fucking doggy style. He pushed back gently, his ass sucking me back in as I withdrew. With each thrust he grabbed my cock with his ass muscles to milk me. The pace was leisurely; we were in no hurry here. I leaned over and nibbled the back of his proud neck. He attempted to turn his head so we could kiss, but all I could do was lick his beard and the corner of his mouth. I picked up speed, felt for his cock and wanked it gently in time to my thrusts, but he took my hand away and said quietly, "Not yet. I want to concentrate on giving you pleasure."

And it was the pleasure he was giving me, that was tipping me over the edge. I had never been able to hold off for so long on a first penetration before in my life and all my pent-up excitement was eager to explode.

"I've got to come soon," I grunted, and Ned began to back up on my cock to meet my increased rhythm. That was it. My cock spewed cum inside Ned's ass, squirting so many times I shuddered with pleasure. The orgasm was so intense it seemed to go on and on so that I thought perhaps I'd hemorrhage spunk until I died.

I collapsed in a puddle of our combined perspiration on his matted back. Ned was the first to move. He disengaged my cock from his ass and lay me down on the sun lounge. He covered me with his body and kissed me gently. "Thanks, I needed that," he said.

"Not as much as I did." I tried to stifle a yawn.

I felt my legs being elevated and my asshole exposed. "Don't," I said softly. "I don't like that." He brushed aside my arms that were feebly attempting to block his passage as easily as he brushed aside my objections.

He lubricated my asshole with the oil, but took so much time massaging and making brief forays internally that I thought he'd accepted my protestations. Yes, a finger would slip in gently without fuss and wiggle about a bit so that it felt good, but I was so warm and relaxed that it scarcely registered the finger was penetrating deeper each time and that eventually it was joined by a companion.

My "mmmm" of contentment gave him the permission he was seeking. He pushed his cock between my cheeks to the door to my bowels. It wasn't until the pain from his initial assault registered with my brain that I realized how far we'd come. I gasped, but it was more a reflex than a reflection of the actual circumstances.

"Relax, Vince," he cooed, lulling me into a comfortable lethargy. He knew what he was doing and slowly penetrated me so painlessly that it came as a shock when I felt his balls slapping against my ass. I had never been fucked like this before. Normally my sex partners rammed at my asshole like invading hordes against a castle wall. Ned had breached my defenses with stealth and perseverance. He was in for the long haul and not the quick spurt of satisfaction.

He rode me slowly at first, so that his thrusts eased me into trusting him totally. Every now and then, he would fuck with increased vigor. I would cry out not in pain but that having a cock in my ass could feel this good. He didn't mistake my vocabulary of sounds. I didn't need to tell him anything; he played my body expertly like a tightened musical instrument. He knew the right movements.

I relinquished control to him. He picked up the pace, filling me with the most extraordinary feelings. I opened my eyes to see that he was watching me carefully, reading his success in my face. I surrendered as his cock began to pick up speed and strength, and although I was not the expert he was, I attempted to imitate the sphincter control he had used. He smiled the first time I did it. He leaned over and stroked the sweat-matted hair from my face.

I was so full of love for this man I had to look away. He didn't misinterpret my action, but caressed my face and began to fuck me with added strength and aggression. I attempted to match him, but he motioned for me to relax. As I did, he continued to dominate me and made my ass feel so good I thought I would blow my load without touching my dick. His breath came in short bursts. I put my hands to his back, attempting to pull him further inside me.

Then he grunted and gave one last thrust. I felt his cum flooding inside me. His mouth flew open and his gasps were my reward for allowing him my ass. He spasmed a few more times, and then with a look of disbelief pulled out and lowered my aching legs. He lay beside me to catch his breath. I held him until his heart stopped beating so violently it threatened to split through his chest.

The late afternoon sun cast its watery heat over us. We were both afraid to speak.

"Can I see you again?" I asked more timidly than I had wanted to sound.

"You mean a date?" he smiled.

"Yea, I guess."

"Something more permanent?" he ventured.

We spent the next half hour discussing our options, and we agreed we knew so little about each other apart from being great at sex that we wouldn't rush it. 'It' being a more permanent relationship. We'd explore the possibility and meanwhile we'd explore each other's bodies with renewed vigor.

And just before we fell asleep together, we agreed that the only problem we could see was how to tell the kids.

# BUMMING A FAG

Banished to the fire stairs for a cigarette in the middle of winter seemed like cruel and unusual punishment to me. But I had reckoned without Damian. My house proud and health conscious boyfriend, Toby, had unilaterally decreed there was to be no smoking in our apartment or even on the open air balcony. It shows you how much I was trying to make this relationship work that I agreed to take my filthy habit outside. What seemed like an okay concession in hot summer months seemed suicidal in the depths of winter, and I had taken to smoking, strictly against the apartment building regulations, on the fire stairs in an effort to stay warm.

That's where Damian found me. The elevator was throwing one of its periodic hissy fits, refusing to budge off the eighth floor, so my little smoker's retreat was in danger of being over-run by a steady stream of cursing residents climbing or descending the stairs to street level. I returned their grumbles while cupping my guilty secret in my hand hoping they wouldn't smell my illicit activity.

"Can I bum a fag, mate?" He startled me because I had not heard him coming up behind me. I was about to turn and tell him not likely with the cost of cigarettes these days and the government soaking smokers for every penny they can prize from our nicotine-stained fingers.

"Sure, mate." I changed my mind and shook the packet until one or two bobbed out. He took one and I lit it with the end of mine.

"I owe ya," he said.

Shit, this kid could owe me any time. Tall, almost six feet, yellow blond hair, probably from surfing or an outdoor job of some kind, slim but not scrawny, biceps that confirmed manual labor, and a sort of rugged, pretty face with lips you just want to slide your cock into.

"Damian," he said after he blew the smoke out of his lungs from a satisfying first drag.

"Brad," I told him.

"Tossed out of your apartment?" he asked, nodding up the stairs.

I sneered. "Yeah. Boyfriend says the ash dirties the carpet. You?"

"Daddy don't like kissing fag breath."

If this kid had a daddy, it weren't no familial relationship – it was more of the sugar variety.

"You work outside?"

"Uh huh," he said.

"I noticed the arms."

"Apprentice brickie. The pay's shit. It's why I have to supplement me wages."

"Sugar daddy?"

"Uh huh."

"Nice way to earn a living." I didn't know what to say. If I'd had visions of this twenty-something twink God being interested in a 5'7", middle-aged, hairy, beer-gutted, billiard-ball bald slob, then they had been well and truly shattered.

He took a long draw of the fag before he answered. "Helps that I'm a slut."

I choked on a lungful of smoke.

"You got the necessaries?" he asked as he crushed the butt under foot.

I fished in my shorts' pocket and brought out a condom and a sachet of lube. Be prepared is not just the Boy Scouts' motto. I never said I was faithful to him upstairs.

Damian took out a mouth spray and gave his throat a coating. He pulled me over and kissed me. It tasted lemony.

"You taste cigarettes?"

"Nah, you're sweet," I said.

He dropped his jeans and bent forward on the stairs.

He looked around at me.

"Don't you wanna?"

I dropped my fag quick smart. "Shit yeah," I said and scrambled out of my shorts and briefs.

My cock had been hard since I first saw him.

"Better make it quick 'cause I'm running late. He hates it if I don't turn up on time."

"You can use the excuse the elevator's out," I said as I ripped open the foil package and sheathed my cock.

"Yeah." Damian pulled his T-shirt up over his back to give me better access. He was like a sculpted god, his tanned skin stretched over taut muscles, with an ass that a man could bury himself in. And I did.

I pushed my fingers in and swirled the lube round his ass band that twitched as I entered him. He was warm, pliable, and inviting. I greased the rubber and pushed my knob against his hole.

"No need to be gentle. I like it rough," he said.

As if to confirm it, he backed up on to my hard cock swallowing me right down to the balls. I held his smooth, boyish back and rammed him hard, my balls banging against his ass. He moved to meet each of my thrusts as if he couldn't get enough cock inside him.

And the tightening and loosening of his sphincter as I plowed inside was dragging the spunk up from my balls.

We weren't in this for the long haul; we could be caught at any moment, and he had an appointment, so I concentrated on fucking the cutest young twink I'd ever had on the end of my cock in I don't know how long. I pinched his nipples, which only made him milk my shaft all the more. I reached under to feel for his prick, but he pushed my hand away.

"Uh uh," he said, and I understood he was saving it for the job ahead.

I pushed him down on the concrete steps and whispered in his ear. "Take it, fucker. Take my hard daddy bear cock in your slutty fuckin' ass!"

He must have been hurting as the edge of the steps bit into his skin, but his groans were more real now and not so faked.

"You won't forget this fuck. Daddy bear fuckin' your tight slut asshole on the stairs. You love daddy's cock shooting his spunk right up inside you, don't you punk?"

"Yes, daddy," he whispered as I shot inside him, my body bucking as the strings of spunk filled the rubber.

He gave me a few seconds to recover and then pulled off my cock. He wiped his ass and dressed quickly. He took the stairs two at a time as he swore, "Shit, I'm gonna be really late. He'll kill me."

I heard him exit three floors above and the door slam behind him as I was still peeling the rubber off my cock.

# FOUR ON THE BEAR FLOOR

"Holy shit, man, get a load of that ass." Jerry focused the binoculars on the fourth floor apartment across the street. With the magnification of those suckers, he could see straight into the living room through the wide-open balcony doors. As wide open as the guy's butthole, if I had my guess.

"Here, let me see." Mike snatched the glasses from him.

"I told you he was something out of the box," I said from the corner bar where I was topping up our drinks. I threw the empty Bourbon bottle in the trash to join the earlier one we'd already polished off.

Jerry, my sleazy boss at Klassic Kars where I worked as a detailer, came back to get his glass. He's chunky, in his early forties, shaven head and a mat of body hair across his chest, across his beer belly; definitely a daddy type, but not exactly "attractive" to go with it. "You weren't kidding, Steve. That guy has it all. I could fuck that."

I knew for a fact that Jerry wasn't fucking anything at the moment. He was always at me to set him up with one of my single friends. It wasn't gonna happen.

Billy sneered. "I don't think there's anything special about him." He hated it when he wasn't the center of attention.

"You're kidding, right?" Mike relinquished the glasses to Jerry, who definitely wanted another look. We'd met Mike at the showroom a few weeks earlier, when he'd come in to give a newly arrived 1956 Buick Century Riviera Four-Door Hardtop the once over. He'd bought it on the spot, counting out the price from a huge wad of high value banknotes he said he always carried in case of emergencies. This guy was seriously wealthy – or a braggart. Maybe both. And dumb as shit to carry around that much cash. Both Jerry and I had pegged him as a definite bear, and Jerry had pegged him as available, something I wasn't, and flirted accordingly. Mike wore baggy blue jeans, navy sneakers and a black cotton tank top that hugged his chest so tight his hard nipples could have poked your eye out if you got too close. It also revealed his hairy muscular arms and the sprout of hair from his chest and also from his back. This guy was seriously hirsute – and proud of it. He looked to be around thirty with shaggy, black hair that he flicked with his fingers to keep it out of his hazel bedroom eyes. I would have been flirting as well, if I hadn't already been in a relationship, although said relationship was as rocky as a row boat in the North Atlantic at the moment. However, we liked to give the outward impression we were the perfect couple.

We had been when we first started out five years before. Billy was the five-feet-eight, tanned skinned, blond haired, blue-eyed beauty with the snug Otter body that had only gotten better and more defined when he'd 'discovered' the gym. I would have said 'obsessed' with the gym since his retrenchment as a sous-chef in a restaurant that didn't survive the economic downturn. That was just one of the problems. I was the other. I'm slightly taller, weightier, and fifteen years older at thirty-eight, with unruly brown hair matched with dirty brown eyes. That's what Billy called them when we first met at a leather bar that was so humid inside we didn't know whether the air conditioning had failed or whether we were so hot for each other we were producing our own power surge.

By the time we'd both emerged from our sex-addled euphoria, we found ourselves saddled with a substantial mortgage on a fifth-floor apartment in a high-rise development full of gay couples and solos, with minimalist but classy furniture, expensive cultural and social tastes, and maxed out credit cards. There is no way we could afford a separation, even if we'd wanted one.

We didn't. We were still comparatively happy together. We fitted, in the parlance of our friends and neighbors. We were popular. A little too popular. The apartment complex was a breeding ground of temptation and infidelity: attractive, buff boys of every color, class, creed and preference – from bears to BDSM to vanilla. I was like a kid in a rainbow hued candy store, and I wanted a taste of all the young cubs. Billy, however, was all eyes front, prim as a Sunday-go-to-meeting front pew fundamentalist.

Trouble is I was finding it hard to, well, always get hard for the same old/same old boyfriend after all these years. No one wants to eat meat and potatoes year in year out, so why would they want to fuck the same ass regardless of how cute? The solution, we'd decided, was Paris, and not because of any overt familiarity with the city, but just a general romantic longing to spice up our lovemaking, which had become as stodgy as porridge. But financially, Paris was as far away as Mars.

That's why we'd been sniping at each other all afternoon, the atmosphere taut as tensile wire across a paddock, when an uninvited and unwelcome Jerry, with two new buddies in tow, arrived for an up-close-and-personal look at our exhibitionist neighbor.

"What's he doing here?" Billy hissed when I told him who had just buzzed our apartment. "You know I can't stand the ugly toad."

"I didn't invite him," I snarled back.

Just then he barreled through the open front door, and we both beamed our best imitation smiles at him. He was too crass to notice, but his buddies did.

"Knew you wouldn't mind," he said. "You know Mike already, and this is his young mate, Raoul. Where're the binoculars?" Jerry was all couth.

Raoul, about the same vintage as Mike, bearded, tattooed and twice as hairy, which equals good looking in Billy's book, had an attitude to match. "If he's as hot as Jerry here says, why don't we go jump him and tattoo his ass with our spunk!" One look through the binoculars was enough to convince him.

"You sure you don't know his number, man? Or even his apartment, so I can go buzz him." Unluckily for Raoul, our neighbor lived in a security building, but that didn't prevent him from shouting obscene invitations across the street to zero success, and to my utter embarrassment.

"You should have bought extra binoculars and installed cinema chairs for the show." Billy was at his sarcastic stage.

"Hey, chill out," Raoul said. "This is some show."

"Tell me about it," Billy said. "I got up the other night for a drink and came out here to find Steve fully naked and jerking off while he watched pretty boy over there in action. He didn't even realize I was watching him until he blew his load in the Zamioculcas zamiifolia. And it's not the first time."

Raoul was getting irritable and horny. "In the fuckin' what?"

"Those plants over there," Billy said, pointing at our Zanzibar ferns.

"Sick, dude," said Mike.

"It's not like I do it every night," I said, trying to placate Billy and keep the evening peaceful. I didn't want an argument in front of the guests. "Anyway his show that night was something else. There was a group thing going on, and I was hard as steel."

"Glad something can still make you hard because it sure isn't me," he said.

"Oh, shiiiiit," Jerry said. "He's got company."

Even Billy moved to the balcony to have a look. Our neighbor never did it in the bedroom, always in the living room, either for our benefit, because he appreciated an audience, or maybe because he never washed his bed sheets. His brazen behavior encouraged mine and I no longer tried to hide the fact I jerked off to him.

Not any more than our little group was attempting to hide the fact we were watching him as closely as teen sci-fi geeks at a Star Trek convention.

Raoul moaned. "That's a great ass, dude. A real furry peach."

"Not what I'd call a great ass," Billy said.

"Fuck, I'd slip him a bit any time," came Jerry.

I tried lightening the mood. "You'd slip anyone a bit any time."

"Just exactly what would you class as a great ass then?" Mike asked with an arch of an eyebrow.

Billy shrugged. "Mine, for example." He patted his butt.

If I'd been honest I would have agreed with him, but in a stale relationship the ass across the street was more appetizing than that readily available in my bed.

Mike laughed. "Yeah, right."

"We'll have to take your word for it," Jerry said.

Billy smiled. "Don't believe me?"

Mike looked from Billy to the exhibitionist across the way. He turned the binoculars on Billy. "I guess Steve will have to be the judge because he's the only one who's seen both."

I was angry our private life was being aired in front of my boss and virtual strangers. "Leave me out of it."

"You'd be biased anyway," Mike chipped in.

"There's only one way to settle this," Raoul said eagerly. "He'll have to show us."

I didn't like where this was heading.

Jerry had turned back to the free show across the street. "Daddy bear is porking his ass. Fuck, that is so hot."

There was a scramble. We grabbed the binoculars from one another for a close up of our neighbor bent over the back of his divan, a hung hairy top pounding him from behind. Even without the aid of glasses, we could see it was quite a performance

"I could give you a much better show," Billy said.

Mike chuckled. "Man, there's no way. That guy is hot. Just look at him."

Lightning fast, Billy had his tank top off to reveal his marbled six pack with the small fluff of blond hair that snaked down under his army fatigues. It was the bane of his life that he couldn't cultivate a thicker pelt. Just as quickly, he dropped his shorts round his ankles. All that separated him from total nakedness was his navy striped briefs that clung to his bulging package and hugged his ass like toffee to an apple.

"Fuck, I thought I was ripped," Raoul said and flexed his arm. His bicep was good enough to lick.

I gulped my bourbon. I was losing control of the situation.

Billy dimmed the lights and programmed the CD player. Suddenly, "Sin" by *Nine Inch Nails* thundered through the apartment. I watched horrified as he slowly gyrated his body and wagged his ass like some cheap pole dancer, miming the lyrics about being 'defaced' and 'disgraced' as he swayed around the room like an Indian cobra under the influence of a Hindu snake charmer. Mike and Raoul were in party mood, whooping and hollering. As my lover swept his hips tantalizingly within reach, Mike opened his wallet and tucked a note into the band of Billy's briefs. Raoul was keen to join the testosterone melee that was engulfing the room and grabbed a handful of cash to shove down the front of

Billy's increasingly revealing underwear while taking the opportunity to cop a feel. Jerry, as usual, was content to sit on his wallet.

I was acutely embarrassed. On the other hand, Billy's eyes shone. Before I could scramble to retrieve his clothing and drag him into the bedroom, even before telling everyone the party was over, he panted and patted his butt cheeks.

He smirked. "Well?"

Jerry adjusted his cock in his pants. I turned away, disgusted.

"Not bad. Not bad at all," Mike said. "But we still haven't seen the real thing."

Jerry sneered. "I can get ass and a blow job anywhere else for what you guys just paid."

Billy extricated the cash from his briefs and flourished it in the air. "You think I'm some two-bit whore?"

But even from where I was seated I could see it was a substantial wad.

Mike dared him by counting out two one hundred dollar bills. "How about this?"

"That's a lot of money just to look at someone's ass," Jerry said. He'd always been a mean bastard.

"What about me, man?" Raoul pleaded. Mike counted out another two hundred.

"You want to see it?" Billy asked Jerry.

The idea of my plug ugly boss ogling my boyfriend's ass turned my stomach. When Jerry hesitated, Mike snapped, "It's only fuckin' money. For that, you get a moment in ass heaven. Or else, you get your money back. Right?"

Billy nodded.

"What about him?" Jerry said, nodding toward me.

"Forget about him," Billy said. "He doesn't matter."

My presence was dismissed so completely, I was momentarily castrated of my balls and my ability to speak.

Jerry thought about it for a split second before reluctantly counting out his cash. "I'm in."

I finally found my voice. "Come on, guys." I tried to push the cash back into their hands, but there were no takers.

Mike smiled. "Hell no, the night just got real interesting."

"Now we can judge for ourselves whether this ass you're always bragging about is as hot as you think," Jerry crowed.

Billy took control. "Get them another drink, Steve. None of that cheap shit either. That good Scotch you save for special occasions."

I poured way too much liquor in their glasses, hoping they'd pass out. Me, I poured an even stiffer one. I gulped it down at once, and it burned my gut like humiliation.

Billy lowered the lights further, small consolation, cleared a spot and had the visitors seat themselves on the floor around the edge of the rug that he was about to use as his stage. To catcalls and whistles, he ramped up the music and *Nine Inch Nails*, his favorite band, spewed out "Closer" as he circled the area, ferociously bumping and grinding to the anthem about wanting to violate, to desecrate, to penetrate, before hooking his fingers in the band of his briefs. Sidelined, I held my breath. Teasing like a professional stripper, Billy slid his hands down until he was stark naked, waving his hard cock close to the visitors' faces. But that's not what they'd paid to see. He swirled around and bent over, parting his perfect muscled asscheeks coated with a fine dusting of blond hair, daring them to touch him while, with perfect timing, he mouthed the lyrics "I want to fuck you like an animal." Raoul had already succumbed to a pheromone rush and was openly stroking his cock in appreciation, while Jerry kept looking in my direction, frightened of any repercussions.

Billy lay back on the coffee table. He raised his legs over his head, spread his butt cheeks with his hands, singing *"my whole resistance is gone"*. All attention focused on his lightly haired thighs leading to that inviting pink, puffy hole. He licked his fingers and started to prod them into his sphincter. He looked so fuckin' hot burying three up to the second knuckle. "I guess I win," he said as he finger fucked the ass I had neglected of late.

I suddenly got my balls back and went to the CD player to end the charade, but in my confusion, all I did was bump the disc up louder. Billy raised his voice over the music, "Are you sure all you want to do is look?"

I could not believe what I was hearing.

"Add another five, and I'll let you fuck me right here."

Mike didn't hesitate. He peeled off five hundred and placed it on the coffee table, then smugly peeled off another five hundred for Raoul. Turning to Jerry he asked, "You in?"

Jerry's lust to pork my lover overcame his natural stinginess. His voice cracked as he told Billy, "Come by my office tomorrow and I'll pay you what you're worth."

The hypnotic song had been edited so that *"I want to fuck you like an animal"* was on a loop, a constant sexual command, cock hardening and orgiastic. Billy writhed to the pulse of the music as Mike spat in his hand to lubricate his prick, then leaning forward, pushed his strong, thin cock against Billy's well-lubed sphincter. He slid right in.

Mike gasped. "Oh fuck."

Raoul moved quickly to hold Billy's legs to give Mike better access. He sank right down to his balls.

"Oh, man, you gotta try this fuckin' hole. Hot as hell, dude. Fuckin' ace."

Billy groaned, a sound I remembered from the first time I pressed my cum-drooling prick inside his eager guts. I shook my head in agony. Mike pulled out, hesitating a split second before lunging back into that slick ass chute. Raoul, not to be denied, slipped his cock into Billy's hungry mouth.

"That wasn't part of the deal," I mumbled.

Jerry was contemptuous. "Who gives a fuck? Always going on about how perfect your fucking relationship is and all the time your boyfriend's a cum dump. Panting for cock from every sick bastard in the neighborhood. Well take a good look when I shove the cock that was never good enough for you up your sweet little boy's fuck hole." Jerry waved his ugly, drooling, stubby cock in my direction.

"This – mouth – was – born – to – suck – cock," Raoul panted. "His – throat – is – slick – as – pure – fuckin' – velvet."

"So is his asshole, man." Mike was battering my lover's ass like a tornado in Kansas. "Sweet asscunt."

"I bet the fuckin' slut could take two in his sweet boy pussy at the same time," Raoul said. "That way we can all do him together."

"I want the fucker's asshole," Jerry said. "No way will I settle for a blow job. This was about his ass."

Mike assumed control. "Okay, but you'll have to take sloppy seconds."

Jerry nodded. "No complaints from me. I'll just get his mouth to slick me up while I'm waiting."

Mike pulled out and lay on the carpet, holding his hard, slimy prick upright so Billy could skewer himself on it, facing the man who was making a whore of him. Once successfully kebabbed, Billy leaned forward to make his ass vulnerable to Raoul's liberally greased, uncircumcised weapon that he squeezed against Mike's, already buried up the battered asshole. Raoul, straining against Billy's elastic ass muscles, made him cry out in pain before he relaxed, murmuring with pleasure. Jerry moved round to the only hole still available. I watched, repulsed, as he forced his thick cock between Billy's lips.

Incredibly, I was harder than I had ever been in my life. Harder than when I jerked off watching our neighbor take cock with considerably less skill than Billy. Harder than when the two of us first met and went at it like proverbial rabbits. Fuck, the realization was like a cartoon light bulb in my brain: I got hard on watching. Sure, I was pissed big time about my lover slutting his body to two strangers, as well as my disgusting boss, but I was more excited than I ever had been when I fucked him. I liked, no, I fuckin' loved watching him take cock in his ass and his mouth. Cocks of strangers. Cock of an ugly brute of a man.

Billy was taking on three, severely stretching his limits. Stretching mine. My cock was feeding directly to my brain, admitting this new experience was the ultimate pleasure. There was no thought about the repercussions of what we were doing to our relationship – was it over? But all anger and frustration left me.

Raoul took over the rhythm of the assfuck, penetrating deeper and deeper, opening Billy wider.

"Fuckin' sensational," he praised as he slid his tan cock along the length of Mike's shaft, Billy's ass muscle stretching to take the two greasy pricks.

Jerry sounded like a bad porn movie as he viciously fucked Billy's mouth. "Fuck the little slut. Bury your cock in his guts. Ram his asshole."

Mike massaged Billy's slobbering cock as he and Raoul raised the momentum. I moved in closer to watch the two amazing slimy, hard pricks shafting their way into the needy hole. It was hot enough to be a porn movie; but knowing it was my boyfriend's ass that was copping a battering sent the sexual mercury through the roof. I was painfully hard. I stripped off my jeans and briefs and began to spit slick my knob. Mike smiled knowingly.

Jerry saw me as well, and encouraged by Billy slurping on his ugly prick like it was prize caviar, kept up his verbal humiliation. "Your sweet slut likes real man cock in his cunt mouth. Watch me slide it down his throat."

Billy didn't seem to care the real ugly fucker he was sucking was my boss, a man with biggest mouth for gossip in the county. It would be all over the showroom tomorrow that he'd fucked my boyfriend. Slamming into Billy's mouth, he held the back of his head, pinning him like a trophy butterfly. "Nasty. Just the way you like, eh boy?" Billy was turning purple from the fat fucker holding his face firm against his belly suffocating him with cock.

Billy gasped for air as gag puke drooled off his lips when Jerry finally let him free. He just wiped his mouth and plunged right back around Jerry's prick. He was oblivious to everything but cock.

The onslaught of Jerry's verbal abuse, plus the friction against his sphincter and his prostate knob buried inside his fuck canal, finally pushed Billy to explode all over Mike's belly. That in turn contracted his ass muscles, squeezing his two synchronized fuckers until they screamed out their pending orgasm and shot almost simultaneously into his guts. They slumped, exhausted, until their shrinking cocks slipped out of Billy's well-fucked hole. Knowing how impatient Jerry was for his turn, they helped Billy back on to the coffee table and went to clean up, all the while keeping a watchful eye on the action.

Billy held his legs apart, his slimy ass canal dripping sex juice and begging to be filled again. Jerry grabbed me by the hair and pushed my face toward his prize. "You always thought this asshole was too good for me. Now look at it." Jerry shoved in his fingers, scooping out cum and forcing it into my mouth. I sucked his fingers clean.

"Too good for anyone but you. Now it's dripping with other fuckers' spooge. Not too good now, is it?" He pushed my face into Billy's crack, smearing my face in the ass spunk. I tasted Mike and Raoul. He yanked my hair again; my face was level with his prick.

"Now get me slicked up Mr. High-and-Mighty. Too fuckin' smug to suck the boss's prick, but now look at you." He shoved it between my lips.

I tried to make him blow so he wouldn't plow Billy.

He must have guessed my intentions because he pushed me away. "That's enough! Beg for it, baby."

Billy whimpered. "Fuck me, fuck me now. I need you inside me,"

"You want my cock, baby? You want my hard man cock?"

"Rape my fuckin' ass! I need cock bad!"

Jerry gave what sounded like a strangled rebel yell and plugged Billy like he was plugging a dam, knocking the wind out of him.

I watched, fascinated, as this ugly fucker rammed into my lover. No finesse, just raw animal fucking.

Jerry cursed the slut, keeping up a string of filthy talk until it became so rancid I knew he was shooting his cumsnot in Billy's asshole. He shuddered the last of his juice into Billy, then pulling out, he wiped his slime over my face.

Now that it was over Jerry could not look me in the eye. He dressed quickly, mumbled his farewell and headed for the door.

Billy lay exhausted, his asshole gaping and dripping spunk. Raoul and Mike, now cleaned up and fully dressed, stood surveying the scene as if it were a disaster zone. I was so shell-shocked by the whole experience I feebly offered them coffee like a good host. They politely turned it down and headed for the door.

"Worth every penny." Raoul adjusted his crotch, and was gone.

Mike hesitated at the door. "He's right you know. One of the best asses I've ever had. You're a very lucky man, Steve. I envy you. And Billy's a lucky man to have you."

When Mike closed the door, the silence was deafening.

Billy lay naked and still, his arm across his eyes, waiting for the storm he knew was coming. I picked up the cash and counted it.

"With that bastard Jerry's money tomorrow that gives us just about enough to take that trip to Paris we were planning for our anniversary." I said, scarcely daring to breathe.

Billy took his arm away from his eyes and looked at me, stunned. I smiled.

He returned my smile. Relieved. He looked at my aching cock. "Why don't you fuck me now."

Damn. We were back to the same old routine. I regretted we'd lost the moment for a new beginning as I slid into his sloppy asscunt.

Then Billy said, "I hear those French boys are really something."

I fucked him with a vigor I hadn't felt for a long time.

# BEAUTY, MATE

What was it that people saw in me that made them think Andrew and I would hit it off? He was gorgeous and the boy most likely to be pursued in a bar. He was intelligent, belonged to various gay political organizations and thought the older generation, of which I was a perfect example, had crippled the gay movement with our hedonism and our lack of political will.

He had flawless skin, if you ignored the little cluster of pimples around this chin – and it was easy to ignore those – a slight blemish on an otherwise perfect complexion. His eyes were what you noticed most. Or was it his smile? His hair, the way it hung over his forehead? Or spiked at the crown?

Here he was hurling abuse at me in public along Oxford Street, Sydney's gay Golden Mile.

"You're so fucking tragic," he screamed as a few guys passed by smirking, probably mentally calculating the difference in our ages ("It's only twelve years," I felt like yelling at them. "He's 20 and I'm 32") and marking me down as a premature sugar daddy. "You don't have an original thought in your fucking head. Everything you say is vomited up from opinion pieces in what passes for quality journalism in this city. It's all shit! You're shit!" To emphasize his point, he threw his arms out to encompass the street on which we were currently the top entertainment. "All this is just commercial bullshit milking the gay proletariat's dollar."

A few people stopped to applaud and, if I hadn't been on the receiving end, I may have applauded as well. But he had the wrong man. He hadn't taken the time to find out. I had marched in gay rights demos in which the police had beaten up protestors. I'd been outside homophobic companies and church diocese when men had been fired for their sexual preference. But, of course, Andrew didn't know that. We'd only met half an hour earlier.

We'd taken an instant dislike to each other on sight.

"Go home, granddad," Andrew said, his energy finally draining out of him. "Your time is gone. Let us take over now."

"It's all yours and you're welcome to it," I bellowed as I slunk away leaving half a dozen predators hovering in hopes of picking over the remains of a friendship that didn't even reach the starter's gate. No one was hovering to swoop over me. Ah, the fickle nature of gay life; and the fickle transience of beauty.

I wasn't ugly. I just wasn't young and beautiful any more.

Back home I slammed the front door in frustration.

"You're home early" Nathan said, getting up to give me a hug as only a long-term boyfriend can.

"Opinionated little prick!" I spat out, and felt better for it.

"Didn't go well then?"

"Thinks he knows everything! Has an opinion, no matter how half-assed it is, on anything I brought up. Oh sure, there's an enquiring mind in back of that pretty little head of his …"

"You didn't say anything to him about his 'pretty little head' did you?"

"I might have."

"You didn't make the mistake of telling him how young he is?"

"Um … well …"

Nathan sighed. "Just exactly how did you take it when people said the same things to you back when you were his age?"

Nathan always did have a way of putting things in perspective.

It was two or three weeks later Andrew and I met again. It wasn't planned. Our house was always open for friendly drop-ins because we were so close to the center of the gay metropolis – for people passing on their way to parties, to the bars, on their way home. Nathan and I had just finished dinner with two close friends when another, Tony, and his entourage turned up at the door. Who should be among that entourage but Andrew. I smelled a rat and suspected Tony was attempting to precipitate another conflagration between the two of us, having heard the gory details of our previous altercation from the bush telegraph that swept Oxford Street.

There was a buzz to the ad hoc gathering, about 10 people in all, not least because of the sudden exploitative interest in Andrew. He was instantly the center of attention, everyone in the room subtly and not so subtly attempting to impress him. There would be heartbreak tonight. One of Andrew's friends had staked a claim and was hovering possessively at his side. I was never a fan of blood sports so I left the room to replenish wines and make coffees and teas.

I was chuckling as I heard voices raised and laughs shrieked with more volume than necessary, people's words tumbling over one another in an effort to dazzle. From my vantage point a room away, it all sounded so shallow and futile.

"Can you do anything?"

The question took me by surprise and I realized only when I looked up that the voices in the living room had subsided. That was because Andrew was in the kitchen speaking to me – quite civilly as it turned out.

"What's the problem?" I asked.

"They all want to fuck me," he said.

I couldn't stop myself from a little payback. "My, aren't we the modest one."

"I should have known," he said as he turned to walk away.

"I'm sorry," I said, and I was. "I know they are. I could hear it from here."

"Any solutions?"

"You'll hurt a few people's feelings," I said.

"That's okay, I seem to manage that anyway." He smiled and that smile said it all.

I dragged him back into the living room and the noise level rose once again.

"Okay, everyone. Listen up," I said in my most authoritarian tone. "Andrew's a bit uncomfortable with all the attention and while he's flattered it does make it awkward. So, how about I go around the room, ask Andrew if he's interested in each of you one at a time, and those who get the nod can slug it out while the rest can just chill out. Okay?"

There was ready agreement. The fear of public humiliation was over-ridden by the hope of anointment.

Very carefully I named each guest, giving Andrew time to weigh up his response, but it was always a warm, but final, 'No,' including to my other half, Nathan.

When it was all over and he'd turned down everyone I said, "Now you can all relax and enjoy yourselves."

I started to go back to the kitchen to finish the drinks when Andrew interrupted. "You haven't asked me about everyone?"

Genuinely puzzled, I asked, "Who didn't I ask you about?"

"You."

Everyone in the room looked at me expectantly. I was the only person who had shown no interest in Andrew. I didn't like whatever game it was he was playing.

"Okay, Andrew. For the record, are you interested in me?"

I'd already turned and was half way down the hall when I heard him say 'Yes.'

I had expected a lot of things, but not that.

People suddenly realized how late it was or how tired they were or else were just so pissed off they couldn't stand it and the house emptied quicker than an inflatable sex doll with a pin hole. Nathan gave me a peck on the cheek and whispered, "Lucky bugger," as he headed off to bed. The only person who resolutely refused to leave was Andrew's leech-like friend. He sat through our desultory conversation and cast a pall over our enthusiasm. It went on for about twenty minutes, him interrupting our very personal snogging with sarcastic observations, most pointedly about my shortcomings.

"Just look at you," he said to me. "Overweight and hairy. Eww."

No amount of hints or straight out requests for him to leave had any effect. We decided our best course was to carry on as if he weren't there. Neither of us had wanted to hurt his feelings, but he was setting himself up for disappointment. Nothing was going to prevent the consummation of our relationship that night.

I looked at Andrew and swept the hair slick off his pale forehead and leaned down to kiss his pimples.

"No one's ever done that before," he said.

I unbuttoned his shirt slowly as I leaned in to kiss him and ran my tongue across his pink lips which he opened to receive me. I gently probed his mouth and sucked in his tongue with just enough force to mean business. I found his nipples and ran my thumb across the little pinky brown nubs. He shuddered as I bent down to lick them and bite them lightly. He was just how I liked my men, hairy. He had a thatch on his chest between his pecs which spread out over his belly, before disappearing under his belt. A regular prairie of body hair.

His cock sprang to attention as I ran my fingers along the outline in his jeans before I unbuttoned them and pulled them, and his briefs, down over his tight fuzzed butt. He peeled off his shirt so that now he was naked. His body was perfection. A swimmer's body, muscular but not overblown.

He just lay, semi-prone, on the settee luxuriating in my stare. He knew he was beautiful and he accepted my gaze as his due. I ran my fingers over his chest and belly deliberately wrapping my fingers in his soft fur, teasing his cock which jolted in expectation of my touch. I turned him over and traced the outline of his spine. His body had the tactile sensation of a beautiful marble sculpture.

I ran my finger between his hairy ass cheeks and sought out his hole. It was moist and I knew it would taste sweet. I parted his legs and pushed my face into the crack, licking the hairs aside in order to ease my tongue into him. He groaned and began to stroke his cock, but I swatted his hand away. I heard the front door close and knew we were finally rid of his friend. Now we could relax fully.

His cock was musky as I ran my tongue around his knob to lick away the light layer of pre-cum, continuing down the ridge under his cock to his balls with their light bush of hair. I sucked them into my mouth to bathe them with my saliva. I worshipped him like priceless porcelain, so careful in case he might break.

But it was all one sided. He lay passive. I was doing all the work. I wanted a little reciprocation. I stood up to strip off my clothes, Andrew watching with interest. He must have liked what he saw because he beckoned me to come back to him. He took my cock in his warm mouth and leisurely sucked me into his throat. It was like velvet. I turned my body to keep pace with him and we both eagerly devoured each other's prick. I couldn't hold off for much longer and he surprised me when he said:

"I like it on my face."

I stood up and over him. He looked so vulnerable.

"Shoot it on me. Blow your load on my pretty fuckin' face," he groaned as he pounded his meat.

I jerked my cock and it didn't take long because his tongue had already brought me so close to the edge. I shot strings of warm spunk across his face, in his hair, and a few squirts went in his mouth open in amazement as his own cock spewed over his stomach.

"Rub it on me," he begged.

I ran my fingers through the puddle of cum in his navel, smearing it across his face and lips. He sucked my fingers clean after I soothed my own cum into his forehead and hair, then I leaned in to kiss him, tasting our co-mingled juices.

"Piss in my face," he said as I got up to fetch a towel.

"Why do you want that?" I said.

"I hate being good looking," he said and I detected bitterness in his voice. "Most guys won't do it. They don't like the idea of defiling beauty. Pissing on me is almost the equivalent to them of defiling a statue in an art gallery."

I picked him up and took him to the bathroom and lay him on the floor. As I sprayed all over his face and his body, his chest hair matting, he smiled his contentment and, in that moment, through the mist of hot piss, he was more beautiful than most people would ever see.

# THERE'S A BEAR IN THERE

I thought nothing of it when I was called up to the Boardroom. I had been there before although not, admittedly, under the new administration. I'd been a favorite of the former CEO, Sir Lionel Cardigan. It was under his benevolent despotism that I'd been employed, fresh out of tertiary college, to front the morning children's program. Twenty years later, I was still there.

"We have something we want to discuss with you," Lionel's son, Frank, said, inviting me to sit at the other end of the gigantic boardroom table that dominated the room, if you discounted the drinks cabinet at which he was helping himself to one of the fine liquors specially imported for his particular tastes. I had been offered coffee. His father would not have approved.

Jennifer Strachan, his personal secretary took minutes of the meeting. She smiled as I entered the room although I knew her well enough to know her welcoming grin hid the hard-as-nails interior that could lop off a whole department at the snap of her fingers. She'd proven indispensable to the youngish Frank when he took over after his father died.

"Let's cut the bullshit here," Frank said, seating himself so far away from me at the opposite end of the huge table that I almost needed to phone my responses through. "Your program's slipping. Has been for some time."

"It's the number one rated children's show in its timeslot," I replied.

"Not difficult when you consider your opposition," Frank said. "We could top the ratings if I went on air reciting the phone book. What do you say, Col?"

Colin Fernbury, the new Program Manager, all-round ass-licker and 'yes' man, nodded sagely. "Research suggests people are looking for more dynamic programming from us. Kids shows are all very well and good—"

"We've won numerous awards for the way we teach numeracy and literacy, we've—"

Frank interrupted. "Yes, yes. Blah, blah, blah with the awards. That's yesterday's news, Bernie. Not what kids today are interested in though, is it?"

He nodded to Fernbury to fill in the details. He picked up a stack of computer print-outs on a very official looking letterhead. "What kids want today, according to our research, is something more technological, more cutting edge, less stuffy, less hidebound, less—"

"Expensive?" I suggested.

"Exactly," Frank agreed, totally missing, or else ignoring, my sarcasm.

"You are the highest paid entertainer in children's television," Fernbury pointed out.

I struggled to keep the indignation out of my voice. "Your father thought I was worth every penny."

"I'm not my father," Frank said coldly.

Fernbury attempted to smooth the waters. "It's not that we think you are worth any less, but the whole company has to tighten its belt. Economic realities and all that. It's not just you we're asking—"

Frank cleared his throat. "Informing."

Fernbury had the decency to appear embarrassed. "Ah, yes, informing."

Frank took over. "Look, mate…"

I shuddered inwardly at the familiarity of the use of the word 'mate.' It could only mean bad news.

"This is a courtesy only, Bernie, because of what you meant to my dad. As soon as this meeting is over, Ms. Strachan will be on to your agent to tell him what we're prepared to offer. I know you did everything on a hand shake from the Old Man, but me, well, I prefer to have it all signed, sealed, and above board." He slid a sheet of paper down the table with a figure on it.

"What's this?" I asked, "Lunch money?"

I saw the edges of Fernbury's lips quiver at the bravado of my question.

"Your new salary as of the first of next month. Take it or leave it."

I dug my nails into the palm of my hand to stop from screaming in anger.

"A bit insulting considering the income from my show has helped save the company's ass on more than one occasion."

"The past is the past, Bernie. I'm sure my Old Man thanked you well enough. This is a whole different ball game. In fact, so you don't have to hear about it from your agent, we're hiring you a new sidekick, a cub bear. The publicity is all set to go. It will bring renewed interest to the show. Wicked new actor. You may have heard of him: Pierce Sweeney."

Frank leaned back in his chair, smug that he'd wiped the floor with me. Everyone had heard of Pierce Sweeney. He stepped straight from his university acting degree into the most popular soap on TV where he'd stayed a year as the pretty boy, buff bod young male romantic lead. People, myself included, watched the program just to see him remove his shirt at least once per episode. It was in his contract.

At the end of the first year he'd traded in a sure income and celebrity magazine publicity to take on Shakespeare with a national company devoted to the classics. His detractors waited for the inevitable scalding reviews of his talent. They were still waiting. His Romeo was acclaimed as the most sizzling audiences had ever seen – his nude scene helped immeasurably – and smaller roles in other Shakespeare plays merely enhanced the 'golden boy' image.

It was sickening to an extent. I had worked all my life for the kudos this young kid was getting. In a moment of clarity once, I looked at myself – really looked – in the bathroom mirror and realized I was getting old. And fat. I was beginning to look as moth-eaten and tired as the bear costume I wore on *If You Go Down to the Woods Today*.

Pierce Sweeney reached the critical and financial stratosphere. There were comparisons with Laurence Oliver, Kenneth Branagh, and others of that elevated ilk when it came to his theatre work, and Johnny Depp, Brad Pitt, and Colin Farrell when it came to his big screen career. The comparisons these days were to Greta Garbo. He'd turned his back on the business and walked away, saying he was sick of the shallow 'assholes' that infested the business. Sick of the millions people made from his talent while he lived on peanuts.

I often wished I could earn such peanuts.

"That's a bit of a comedown, isn't it?" I asked.

"Who gives a shit what it is?" Frank replied. "All I know is it's good for publicity. It'll give that dead carcass of a show of yours a boot where it needs it."

"But no one will see him. It could be anybody under that bear suit."

Frank crowed triumphantly. "Exactly my point. Oh, we'll make sure there are plenty of shots of him getting his make-up applied, costumed up to the neck in his bear skin, all that sort of shit. Everyone who watches the program will know there's a top class actor under all that fur. They won't care who's prancing around in your costume. Anyone could play it, the audience simply doesn't care."

I understood the threat.

"Speak to your agent, Bernie," Frank soothed. "I'm sure he'll talk sense. Don't take too long to make up your mind."

With that I was dismissed. I had my hand on the door to the Boardroom. "I presume you and the other members of the Board are taking a commensurate cut in your very generous salary and perks package?"

The glass shattered against the door as I shut it behind me.

As it transpired, my agent, Howie Taurog, was sympathetic up to a point. "Bernie, baby, it's good to see you" he said, not bothering to rise from behind his enormous mahogany desk, the size of which didn't come close to matching the size of his ego. "Your boss has been in touch." He tapped a pile of papers on his desk although I could see from the letterhead, even upside down, that it had nothing to do with me or the television station that employed me. Howie was all show. If he hadn't been such a successful agent, he could have been an actor.

"They're shafting me, Howie. Bringing in Pierce Sweeney to be my offsider."

He whistled. "I heard rumors. I thought they were just that. The kid hasn't been seen in eighteen months or more. Word is he's a crack addict, a boozer, psychotic, gone to fat, you name it. I guess we'll see."

"Bit of a comedown, isn't it?"

"Good for you though. It'll give the show a profile with the media that it's never had before. I'll ring around, see if I can get you a couple of interviews. What you think of the new kid, the revitalization of a stale concept, that sort of crap."

Maybe the show had gone a bit stale after all these years. If Howie thought so, it had to be true. He didn't pull his punches.

"It's a big cut in salary."

"Not negotiable," he admitted. "On a take-it-or-leave-it basis." He shrugged. "Certainly a slap in the kisser for someone with your track record, but things are tough all over, Bernie. I hear even Frank is tightening his belt."

I couldn't help sounding bitter. "What? One less hooker during his notorious afternoon siesta?"

Howie choked on his guffaw, trying to look stern and failing miserably. "That sort of attitude is not helpful, Bernie."

"Spare me the hypocrisy," I snapped. "Your only concern is that your cash bear is about to dry up because, let me tell you, Howie, the way they're treating me…" I left the threat unstated, knowing he would prefer ten per cent of what little they were now offering as opposed to ten per cent of nothing.

"It's not a good time to be out of work, Bernie."

"It's not like you've managed to find me many jobs during my twenty years of playing Papa Bear to a bunch of kids."

"I thought you liked the gig?"

"I did. I do. I just don't like the way I've been taken for granted. They think because I'm done up like a giant fur ball that it doesn't take talent. Let me tell you, Howie, it takes even more talent to animate a bear suit than if I was stone cold naked."

"Hey," he said, throwing his hands up in surrender. "You don't have to convince me. Don't shoot the messenger. I'll do my best for you, mate." There was that word again. "But I'm battering my head up against empty coffers."

"Do your best, Howie. Do your fuckin' best."

"It's what you pay me for."

"Then start looking around for movie projects that may suit me."

"Have you looked at your CV lately, Bernie? Twenty years of playing Bernie the Bear doesn't exactly equip you as leading man material."

"I got great reviews for my stage work."

"Twenty years ago, Bernie, when you were twenty stone lighter."

Yeah, he was exaggerating, but it still hurt because there was an element of truth to it. I'd grown to look like my character.

I was in a bad mood all the way home. How dare they treat me like this. If it hadn't been for me, the kids program never would have made it past the first season. The Old Man knew that. He knew to scratch where it itched. Of course, as Frank said, that was all in the past. But, damn it, I believed in those old-fashioned virtues like loyalty.

I'd taken myself to the bathroom, stripping off my clothes to take a really good look at myself. I'd let myself go, no doubt about it. You didn't need to look your best when you spent your mornings in a television studio hidden beneath acres of brown fur. So I didn't take so much care over what I ate and what I drank. Sure, I got a beer belly but that helps me get in character. Maybe I could get myself some laser treatment. Get rid of some of that fur on my back but it sure does help my character. So does the beard. That's neat at least. Do bears wear beards? If I wasn't such a committed actor I'd go to the gym, lose all those extra pounds, get the body hair off, and go to a decent hairdresser instead of looking like a lumberjack all the time. As for those plaid shirts…

Who was I kidding? This was me. This was the real me. I was no swashbuckling leading man. I couldn't recite Shakespeare for shit. I'd stayed where I was because I was scared I'd end up just another washed up actor on the slag heap at fifty with a few commercials and character parts to look back on. Besides, I was good at what I did. Kids love me. I have a natural rappaw…get it? Don't rub it in, humor's not my strong suit, although kids think I'm a riot. That's based on my shape, not my verbal dexterity.

Oh, Bernie the Bear speaks. I wear the bear costume from the neck down. In the early episodes – available now on DVD for which I'm getting a pittance in royalties, thank you very much, Howie – I wore a bear costume head. You can see the kids shy away thinking I'm a real bear. It was hard for me to react to them so after five or six episodes it was decided to try it with my own head. That's when the producers asked me to let my hair grow, later adding a beard. You can see the pizza and the beer putting the weight on me over the years just by purchasing the complete boxed set of the series – $59.99 plus postage with a free Bernie the Bear stuffed toy thrown in for good measure if you're amongst the first fifty to purchase after the ad appears on TV.

At least I got a set for free. With a Bernie the Bear that looks absolutely nothing like me. It looks as if the line of soft toys is about to be joined by…Benji the Bear Cub, as it turned out.

Frank wasted no time in installing the newest bear on the block and it was obvious who was receiving the royal treatment. It sure wasn't me.

When I turned up for work the following Monday, my dressing room had been seconded for use by the newest edition to the clan. My way was barred as I attempted to enter my own dressing room by the most officious woman I have ever met.

"Who are you?" she snapped, screwing up her nose as she examined me from top to toe as if I were some sort of smelly garbage. "I don't have time to waste on you; I'm getting Pierce Sweeney, the new star of this show, ready for his publicity shots. Now move along before I have you removed."

My voice trembled with anger. "You're in my dressing room."

"My, aren't we the proprietorial one?" she sneered. "But, for your information, we've taken over today in order to get Pierce Sweeney ready."

"I'm on air in less an hour, where am I to get into costume and make-up."

"Oh," she said, not even having the decency to apologize for her numerous gaffes. "I think we put your smelly old stuff over..." she looked about, then pointed her witch-like claw at a makeshift table and mirror that had been set up to one side of the sound stage, "...there."

A voice from inside, called, "Who is it, Stella?"

The harridan looked over her shoulder and replied, "Nobody."

I opened my mouth to say something but she'd closed the door in my face before I'd even drawn breath.

Storming off to find Nolan, the floor manager, I was shaking so much I could scarcely speak when I found him. I didn't have to.

"I see you've met the Wicked Witch of the West."

"She's commandeered my dressing room. Who is she?"

"Yes, I know, Bernie. I'm sorry. Orders from above. Her name's Stella Willoughby. Frank appointed her as personal assistant to our new young cub. She's managed to rub everyone up the wrong way and she's only been on set for two hours. If you can bear with it for today, everything should be back to normal by tomorrow. By the way, you're needed for a photo shoot with your new assistant after today's show. I've been instructed to inform you to hang around."

"How am I supposed to do my own make-up in a dark corner, and where, pray tell am I to…?" I mimed pissing.

Nolan's face dropped. "See that bucket?"

I closed my eyes and counted to ten. Then twenty, then thirty. By the time I reached forty I was sure the sprinkler system would activate I was so steaming.

"They want me to walk, don't they?"

"Yup," Nolan answered succinctly. "That would be my guess."

I trusted his opinion because he'd been with the show almost as long as I had.

"I wouldn't blame you if you did, Bernie. The way they're treating all of us old hands is disgusting. But I got two kids, I can't afford—"

"Hey, don't sweat it on my account. If the situation were reversed, I'd feel the same way. You do what you have to."

"I'll see if I can get Gloria to help with your make-up," he said, heading off in the direction of my former dressing room. He came back a few minutes later, his tail between his legs. "No luck. Cruella De Vil won't let her go."

I'd already attempted the impossible at the makeshift table and chair with the wobbly leg, the mirror almost falling and shattering on the floor.

"Look at this," I said, showing him how awkward the seating was.

"You want me to get Reg?"

"I think it's time," I said.

Nolan smiled. "Good boy."

Reg was a friend to all us jungle creatures that populated early morning television. He was our actor's union rep. He wouldn't stand for any nonsense. I sat patiently on a more stable packing case while I waited, watching the clock tick closer to show time. I'd never once missed an entrance. Fortunately, *If You Go Down to the Woods Today* was on delayed telecast. We began about half an hour before actual broadcast time which allowed us time to edit any glitches in the program. It was still mighty tight but better than having a child throw up or shit themselves in fright on air.

Reg was a bull of a man who usually played heavies and mobsters in teleseries but loved his work on the show that followed mine as the dumb ass sidekick of Rocket Roger. He was as gentle as a lamb with the ferocity of a bear when he was crossed. After I'd explained the situation to him, he was mighty pissed off.

"I heard about the broom sweeping a new path through early morning TV," he commiserated. "You're the last person I thought it would affect. Don't they realize you're the bread and butter to this organization?"

"I'm not asking for any special privileges, Reg. You know me, I'll muck in with the best of them but look at this." I showed him the bucket, and my dressing table.

"Health and safety, Bernie. I'm instructing you not to sit at that booby trap. If anyone tries telling you otherwise refer them to me. You say they won't let you in your own dressing room?"

I nodded.

"Then, I suggest you just wait here while I see what I can do. I know Frank is watching the monitor in the Boardroom with prospective sponsors waiting to meet the new cub. I'll have a word in his shell-like. And, if I may make a suggestion about the bucket."

I laughed. It was the first time since I'd arrived at work that morning.

Word got around the set about my stand. I received numerous back slaps of support plus a few hissed catcalls about 'intransigence.' While I waited for the shit to hit the fan, I calculated my financial situation on the back of an old envelope I found on the floor. I wasn't wealthy, but I'd invested well and had enough to live comfortably, if not extravagantly, for years if need be.

I didn't fancy being out of work, acting was my lifeblood, but if you let them treat you like shit then they'll trample you underfoot.

It took until ten minutes past start-up time before there was a buzz among the floor crew. They knew what was going on. It must have taken that long for it to filter upstairs. Nolan was standing beside me when he took a call from a Frank so incensed that his unofficial launch of the new cub was compromised I heard him from where I was standing.

"Yes, Mr. Cardigan, I understand but until Bernie can get into his costume and apply his make-up we can't begin."

While sounding totally apologetic and subservient, Nolan managed to plaster the wickedest grin across his face. It comes with practice. His job entailed kowtowing to management while being on the workers' side.

"Because, Mr. Cardigan, Ms. Willoughby is in Bernie's dressing room with Mr. Sweeney and has barricaded the door. She won't allow anyone to enter. His costume is in there and he needs Gloria to do his make-up."

I could hear Frank's expletives turning the air blue just before he hung up the phone. Nolan and I high fived, our eyes turned expectantly toward the door to my dressing room. We'd counted up to eight before it opened and a red-faced Ms. Willoughby headed toward us.

"I'd stand to one side if I were you, Nolan," I advised.

Reg appeared out of nowhere, as support in case things got ugly.

"This should be good," he nudged.

Stella Willoughby was not gracious in defeat. If anything, she was even more antagonistic and sarcastic. "We've finished with the dressing room," she said bluntly.

"Which dressing room?" I pressed.

She wasn't going to fall for that. "The dressing room we were using."

"Whose dressing room?"

"For fuck's sake, stop playing these childish games."

"I hope you left it in the condition you found it, as I can't concentrate and I become very agitated if it isn't in a pristine state."

How do you spell mortification, Ms. Willoughby?

"Well, we tidied up as best we could but under the circumstances you'll have to make do," she sneered.

"Oh," I said as nice as pie. "Like I had to make do with this jerry-built disaster here. Which reminds me. That coffee I had earlier needs to come out." I unzipped and dragged my flaccid cock from my trousers. Ms. Willoughby drew back in surprise but suddenly found herself hemmed in by Reg and Nolan. I aimed rather haphazardly at the bucket and began to piss. I'm sorry to say a good deal of it missed the rim of the bucket, splashing against Ms. Willoughby's rather expensive-looking dress skirt and onto her even more expensive shoes. Try as I might, I just didn't seem to get my aim right until I shook the very last drops off the head of my cock and tucked it away.

"Let's have a look at my dressing room, shall we?" I said brightly, standing far enough away from the fuming harridan that she couldn't reach me with her claws. She attempted to walk away but Reg took her by the elbow to steer her along with us.

All things considered the dressing room was in pretty good condition. However, that wasn't about to stop me.

"No, no. This simply won't do. I can't work in this squalor." I ran my finger across the make-up table and a little powder and blush adhered to my finger. I held it up for inspection. "Look at all the rubbish on the floor." There were about a half dozen tissues lying about under chairs and other out-of-the-way places. Most likely, they were mine.

Frank must have put the fear of god into Ms. Willoughby because she got down on her hands and knees, fossicking under furniture to retrieve the rubbish. It was cruel but no worse than the manner in which she had disrespected me. I was making an implacable enemy but if she was the future then there was no role left for me in television.

When she'd crawled around the floor long enough so that the smell of piss began to get in our nostrils, I dismissed her with, "For heaven's sake, go and wash, Ms. Willoughby. You smell like a latrine."

With Gloria's help, I made it onto the set with six minutes to spare. I gave that show everything I had. I was magnificent. The kids loved me, the guest stars sparkled, I was so high on my minor victory that I was unassailable. At least until the theme song and the end credits.

I was pumped as I shook hands with the crew. They realized something was up. When I went back to my dressing room, the young cub was waiting for me. People expected fireworks, and they got it.

Pierce's eyes flashed as I entered and sat to remove my make-up. He was shaking, but managed to keep his voice from breaking. He took a deep breath, then launched his attack. "To think I used to admire you, Mr. Everson. I watched you as a youngster on TV. I never thought I would ever work with the great Bernie the Bear. And here you are. One of the rudest, most vulgar individuals imaginable. I never expected it of you of all people. You've crushed a fantasy of mine. You've reduced a sensitive woman to tears with your behavior."

Yeah, I'm afraid he droned on and on in a similar vein. I had no intention of enlightening him to the true facts rather than the facts as relayed by Cruella. Sure, I was vulgar and uncouth. I was fighting for my now non-existent career. It was childish – but, god, it felt so good.

I interrupted Pierce mid-accusation as I looked into his eyes in the mirror as I removed my make-up.

"Mr. Sweeney," I said over the top of him. "You have the uncanny knack of managing to remain beautiful even in anger. That's a rare ability. You will go far."

It threw him for a moment, but he shook his head in disgust before pushing his way out of the dressing room. He really was a remarkably good looking young man. He'd obviously filled out in the face; the body I couldn't see because he was already in costume for the photographs. I was saddened that I would never get to know him better as a co-worker because I knew with absolute certainty that there was no one of any note in management who would be on my side.

I packed up my few personal items, thanked Reg and Nolan for their support and wished them the very best of luck. They'd both need it. By the time I drove my car to the gate, Bert in security had been instructed to ask for my gate permit.

"Sorry, Bernie," he said.

"That's okay. I had a good run."

As I drove off, he waved, calling, "I'll miss you, Bernie. And those lousy jokes of yours."

I didn't have to get up early in the morning, so I drank myself into oblivion, letting the constant intrusion of phone calls go through to voicemail.

*I vant to be alone.*

What I wanted the next morning was aspirin by the bucket. My head hurt. My gut hurt. And, sure as fuck, my career hurt when I opened the morning newspaper which I had delivered to my door. In big letters on the entertainment page was the headline, FUR FLIES ON THE SET OF KIDS SHOW.

I perused it briefly. As expected it had been written by one of the hacks at the newspaper Frank owned. Management had obviously fed their side of the story so that I came across as a drunken oaf who flashed his dick in front of an innocent and shell-shocked Ms. Willoughby. The crew would set about setting the record straight throughout the industry although the general public would lap up the scandal and believe every word they read. It was the nature of the beast.

Frank could not have wished for better publicity. People would tune in this morning to watch major star Pierce Sweeney fill my paws. Good luck to him. I wouldn't be watching. I could not appraise his performance dispassionately. It would be weeks before I'd be able to do that. Besides, my friends and acquaintances would fill me in.

I'd finished skimming the story when my cell phone rang. I could tell from the ring tone it was Howie. Better to get it over with now. No point in allowing it to fester. He surprised me.

"I suppose you've read this morning's papers," he said.

"No, Howie, I just got up and I'm having coffee."

"You're big news, Bernie. Bigger news than you've been in the past ten years. The phone hasn't stopped with offers. Some of them might even appeal."

"Not now, Howie. I'm heading up the coast for a little 'me' time."

Early in my illustrious career, I'd bought a modest holiday home at Bilby Beach, a few hours north of the city. Because of its unusual geographical lay-out, there was a scarcity of land that could be used for building. As a result, the village was left pretty much alone, developers having nestled in larger areas where the profits could be maximized. I had bought in just before prices sky-rocketed.

I never managed to get away more than a few weeks a year, usually over the Christmas/New Year period when my program was on hiatus. I did love it there. My house was high up on the hill overlooking the main street. From the back verandah, I have access to the sandy beach, or the deck on which I can sit and read and watch the human traffic go by, sometimes even inducing a passing male minnow or two into my bed. I've been particularly fortunate in attracting surfer boys, still fluid in their attraction to other humans.

It helped that they spread the word that my throat was like velvet and sucked better than any Hoover on the market. Plus, I swallowed.

The locals knew me well enough, particularly Sally who ran the Post Office/general store where I collected my mail and my groceries, and Kevin and Cec, two older queens who ran the small café/restaurant/burger joint, with whom I'd shared many a comforting evening when I was younger and more to their taste.

"Don't disappear for too long, Bernie. People forget very quickly." Howie advised

"Tell you what. Give me two to three weeks while you sort the offers out. See if any of them are genuine. I don't care how down-market or unusual. In fact, the more outrageous the better. Come up and spend a weekend. Wind down. Relax. We can discuss what's on offer. Then we can plan."

"You know relaxation is as foreign to me as a good pair of women's breasts are to you. But, for you I'll drive up and stay overnight. How's that?"

"Best offer I've had in weeks."

"I'll be in touch," Howie said. Just before he hung up, he said, "You did good, Bernie. They treated you like shit. I'm proud of you for walking away."

I had tears in my eyes as I put the phone down.

After I'd showered and shaved, feeling almost human again, I listened to the voicemails which were mainly a cross-section of congratulations on my stand, although a few worry warts wondered what the future held for a man who knew nothing but acting like a bear. I deleted them all without ringing back. They could wait.

I packed enough to tide me over for a few weeks, stowed my bags in the SUV and took off, my body not quite believing it was free to do as it pleased. I made good time up the expressway until I turned off on to the scenic coast road which wound like limp strands of spaghetti around the coastal mountains through the forests of gums and mangrove swamps as I got closer to my destination.

Bilby Beach always made me smile when it appeared spread out before me as I crested the hill into the town. It was straight off a postcard. Or else, if one had a twisted sense of humor plus a touch of the macabre, one of those quiet resorts that would make a perfect setting for a horror movie with the invasion of aliens, or flocks of murderous birds, or ravenous sea creatures. I felt at home here. At least for a few weeks, after which the loneliness and the lack of companionship drove me back to the city. It had long been my heart's desire to carry a man I could possibly share my life with over the threshold. To date, there had not been anyone even remotely worthy of it.

Not for want of trying. Especially in my younger days before the hair sprouted all over my body like the wild grasses on the nearby dunes. I'd cared at first, cared incredibly, until I discovered there were as many men out there who liked hairy pelts as the men who didn't like body hair. Unfortunately both camps shared a common fault, they were just as shallow and uninteresting as each other. Every now and then I'd meet a man who was a possibility for a long-term commitment but something always got in the way: my career or his, my bad habits or his, things too countless to enumerate and much too trivial to remember.

I stopped off at Sally's store, greeted by shrieks of surprise and the warmest hug ever, to stock up on provisions and to let her know I was in town. She had a spare key to the cottage as she looked after it while I was absent, ensuring it withstood the ravages of the salt spray from the ocean as well as the ravages of surfers who attempted to break in from time to time thinking it would provide comfortable free accommodation. Rarely had she been forced to seek police intervention.

My first task was to fling open all the windows and the door onto the back verandah to allow the light and the cool breeze access. Taking a deep breath, I felt at peace. The panic could wait. I poured myself a cold drink from the store and shucked my shirt before hoisting myself into the hammock after I had released it from where I kept it bolted to the ceiling on the verandah.

Ah, I'd forgotten how good it could be when you slowed down and let life catch up with you. I was feeling lazy, so later as the sun sank into the ocean, I strolled down to Kevin and Cec's for a burger and chips. Not good for my figure but who did I have to look my best for? I chuckled. I no longer had to keep my bear shape. I could do what I liked. But you know what? I'd actually grown comfortable with my body over the past decade or so.

I didn't want to be like all those skinny pretty boy actors and models. I didn't want to have to put in those excessive hours crunching and stepping and pumping at the gym. I was round, I was hirsute, fuckin' get used to it or get off my porch.

Cec made burgers just the way I liked them: smothered in caramelized onion with two slices of cheese and extra beetroot. I swear he also made the best chips in the country. I could have murdered a second serving but I didn't want to go back to the cottage bloated. Instead, I strolled through the car park to sit on the sand, eerie in the moonlight, looking out to sea, the sound of the somnolent waves casting up on the shore barely disguising the moans and yelps of couples making out in the darker recesses among the dunes.

A young blond surfer joined their cries of pleasure as I sucked his strong hard cock until I drained all the juice from his balls. He didn't reciprocate; those boys never did. For a few short moments, however, I had human contact. Strangely, it left me dissatisfied. Sure it was a boost to my ego that I could pull such a cute young guy, although I suspect I was little more than a wet receptacle for his sperm. He didn't choose me for my looks or my personality, he chose me because I was convenient. Besides, I had no one to whom to boast of my conquest.

I went back to the cottage and jerked off to the image of the young surfer spread-eagled on the bed in front of me as I plowed his blond furry ass. I wonder how he'd feel if he could read my fantasy?

I woke the next morning thinking I was late for work before the caw of circling seagulls reminded me of my predicament. I wasn't used to leisure; it didn't sit comfortably on me. Instead of busying myself with preparing breakfast, I headed down to Sally's to see what paperbacks she had in stock. I knew it would be a desultory collection of yesteryear's best sellers. I had to get myself an eBook reader or a tablet, that way the world was my library.

Sally made coffee you could pave a road with – just the way I like it - and I knew she'd be brewing up a batch of liquid caffeine and would invite me to share a cup or two. As we sipped the heart starter, she filled me in on the town's scandals and interesting happenings – none – and I carefully avoided her questions about the 'misunderstanding' on the set of *If You Go Down to the Woods Today*.

She read the papers. Bilby Beach was abuzz with reports of my behavior; after all, I was their most famous resident. How small town can you get?

I knew she wouldn't let go until I told her my side of the story. She tutted her support as I spread it out before her, embellishing a little here, censoring a little there. I knew that telling Sally was as good as having it on the front page of a city newspaper. It would be all over town by the end of the day. At least they would hear my side of the affair, unlike the readers of the city dailies, the entertainment writers of which were beholden to Frank Cardigan for their living so were very keen to tell his 'official' version of events.

So the first week passed. I pretended I was enjoying myself but, without someone to share my little hideaway, I was restless. The limited opportunities for conversation in the village were not enough to keep me stimulated and I was in danger of falling comatose by the side of the road, rigid with boredom.

Normally, in such a situation I would have fled back to the city and the security of work. Not anymore.

The end of the business week brought respite insofar as the sudden influx of weekenders to the area. They brought a certain excitement that was an antidote to the Monday-to-Friday calm. But even that was not enough to offset the ennui that enveloped me. On Saturday morning I bought all the weekend newspapers to read the book reviews, the travel section, and I did peek at the entertainment pages and interviews. One of the color supplements had a full-page pic of Pierce Sweeney with the banner: Is this taking Method Acting too far?

It was a startling cover and I flicked open the magazine to discover another half dozen pictures of Pierce in and out of his bear costume. The photos of him in character for his role as Benji the Cub Bear were official shots, the photos of him in his shorts, sunbathing in the garden of one of his homes were obviously taken by paparazzi.

The unspoken question the photographs begged was: what happened to the muscular, smooth Pierce Sweeney? The photos revealed a chunky, hairy bear of a man. Not unattractive at all – in fact, hot as Hades – but not the gorgeous smooth twink that had set many a male and female heart aflutter.

An enterprising journalist had brazenly rung Mr. Sweeney about his appearance and was promptly abused for his troubles. His personal assistant was more forthcoming. Ms. Willoughby had obviously prepared for such an eventuality and had carefully scripted an answer which had just enough plausibility to make it believable.

"Mr. Sweeney is an actor dedicated to his art. Dedicated to truth in performance. He follows the Stanislavski Method. He finds the way to the core of the character is to transform his body to the character he's playing as much as possible."

I felt like yelling, "He's playing Benji the Bear Cub, for fuck's sake! How much method do you need for that?"

From the reviews of his first week on the show, the Method obviously wasn't working too well. The critics were lukewarm to scathing, although all of them held fire on totally panning him because of his sudden ascent to the throne I'd abdicated so unexpectedly. It was ironic that people who'd never given me a moment's thought in print were now expressing opinions that my Bernie the Bear was the Olivier of children's television acting. I would have cried if I hadn't been laughing fit to get a stitch in my side.

Okay, I'm only human. I tuned in on Monday to watch him. He was awkward, he seemed uncomfortable around the kids on the show, and he looked miserable. Management had obviously dug up another actor to help him out. There was a new Bernie the Bear but the kids were a wake-up and one young boy kicked the actor in the shins in disgust, shouting, "You're not Bernie the Bear." I didn't care about the actor who'd taken over my role but Pierce was floundering. I searched through my contacts and phoned Nolan on the set after the show finished.

After we swapped a few pleasantries and commiserations – Nolan said the atmosphere on set was poisonous – I suggested he tell Pierce not to be so patronizing to the children. They could easily tell when an adult was talking down to them.

"Tell Pierce to treat them as little adults and they'll react better."

Nolan assured me he would not reveal that I was the person who'd proffered advice, as Pierce would find it highly suspect and accuse me of sabotage. Pierce was better the next day. Call me an old busybody but I didn't want to see the lad fail. For the remainder of the week, I left anonymous tips for Pierce via Nolan. By Friday, Pierce was finding the right rhythm and the kids were warming to him although there still moans of "We want the real Bernie the Bear."

The few journalists who bothered to mention Pierce at all that week noted his improvement, one even going so far as to ascribe it to a mysterious 'friend' who rang after each episode to critique the show. Pierce, and the station, would neither confirm nor deny the rumor.

The following Monday, another actor had been roped in to play Bernie, but he was equally as woeful as his predecessor and the children were so antagonistic it threatened to degenerate into a free-for-all. I did the inexcusable. I rang Nolan while the show was on air, advising him how Pierce could put a lid on the disruption and restore calm. During a commercial break, he obviously passed on the advice because Pierce corralled the kids into good behavior.

By Wednesday, I'd run out of things to pass on to improve his performance, and by Friday Benji the Bear Cub was on top of his game. It gave me a certain sense of satisfaction to know I'd helped although, in the process, I'd cut my own career throat.

Look, I don't know why I did it. The kid was the 'enemy.' I should have wanted to see him and the show fail, but I just couldn't. I'd worked so hard for twenty years to make it work and even now I couldn't bear to watch it falter.

I determined to let it be now that it had improved sufficiently that it didn't need me hovering over it like God. Besides, late Friday evening I received a visitor. Not Howie, whom I had been expecting but who canceled at the last minute.

I was lying on the lounge sipping a superior white wine, quite mellow under its influence, watching an old movie on the flat screen in the living room. I saw his outline reflected in the screen and knew immediately who it was. He'd come in via the back verandah because the doors were wide open. He must have seen me tense, for he said, "Mind if I join you?"

"Do you really want to mix with such a vulgarian?" I asked, without shifting.

"Look, I'm sorry about that. I didn't know the full story," he pleaded.

"You always go off half-cocked?"

"Not if I can go off fully cocked."

"That was pretty feeble," I said, without rancor.

"Look, I drove like the clackers to get here. I can say my piece and go if you like. Or we can have a conversation, painful as it will be for me, and I can try to make it up to you."

I retrieved the remote control and clicked off the telly, finally turning to face him.

"What is it you want?"

"May I sit?"

I nodded and he parked his body at the opposite end of the lounge.

"Would you like a drink?"

"Not on an empty stomach, I'd be silly in about half an hour."

"In that case, follow me."

I led the way to Kevin and Cec's. It served a two-fold purpose. I wouldn't have to listen to whatever it was he had to say, especially if it was personal or abusive, until he and I both had our stomach's lined. If we were going to drink late into the evening, spilling our guts, I didn't want a hangover the next day.

Pierce licked his fingers in appreciation of Cec's culinary skills, downing his diet soft drink, burping loudly enough that the parents of kids around us glared while the kids chortled and attempted to imitate him.

He patted his stomach, a look of total satisfaction on his face.

"Nolan told me it was you."

"I asked him not to."

"I had to get him drunk before he loosened his tongue."

"He's a good man."

Pierce nodded. "Yes, he is. It's taken me a little while to work out the goodies from the baddies. I made a few mistakes in the beginning. "

"For instance?"

"Stella Willoughby, for one."

"Mmm."

"You, for another."

I got up. It was obviously time for The Talk. That was better done in private.

Waving goodbye to Kevin who pottered around behind the front counter, we headed back to the cottage.

"What about me?"

"Can I lay my cards on the table?" he asked.

"If it's important to you."

"I never wanted to take over your show. I didn't know the plans Frank Cardigan had for me. I think his ideas are shit. He should never be allowed to make artistic decisions."

"Amen to that."

"I wanted to appear on the show, maybe for a season or two, that's all."

"Why? With your talent and your looks you had the world at your feet. You don't have to appear on children's TV. You could move to Los Angeles or London. You'd have agents and producers lining up."

"I needed a break from the celebrity circuit. It was doing my head in. People were more interested in my looks or who I was sleeping with, they never wanted to talk about my acting. That's what's important to me."

"I'm impressed. Most guys with your advantages would be laying every hot chick they can get their dick into."

He ignored me.

"The main reason I wanted to…" I heard his sharp intake of breath before he continued, "I admire you and wanted to work with you."

I turned to look at him to see if he was baiting me but he appeared deadly serious.

"Why would you want to work with me?"

"Because you're the man who encouraged me."

"Encouraged you?"

"I used to watch you on TV when I was little—"

"Way to make me feel old."

"Don't interrupt me or I may have to teach you some manners."

"Promises, promises."

"Right." With that he drew back his beefy hand and swatted me on the ass.

It stung, but it was the fact that he did it which most surprised me. I looked at him, the crooked smile on his lips, the superior stance as he waited for my reaction.

"I dare you to do that again."

"Oh, I'll do it again. And again. Over and over until you beg me to stop."

He grabbed me in a headlock and with his free hand swatted my ass until I felt the blood tingle in my butt cheeks.

I struggled so he let me go. He was as flustered in the cheeks as my ass felt.

"You're fuckin' gay, aren't you?" I said.

"What makes you think that?" he asked, pulling me to him and sealing his lips against mine, pushing his tongue into my open mouth, lathing my teeth with his saliva.

We had to separate in order to breathe.

"Is it the way I kiss?" he asked. "Is that what gives me away?"

I stared into his eyes, attempting vainly to read him. "If this is some sort of set-up, I will truly never forgive you."

"This is no set-up, Bernie. I've been hot for you all my adult life."

"Has Frank put you up to this to lure me back on the show, because if he has…" I never got to complete the sentence because Pierce stopped the words with his tongue. I felt his cock pressing into my thigh as he hugged me as close to him as I could get without being inside him.

"How about that drink now?"

We raced each other back to the house, chiacking all the way.

I opened a new bottle and filled two glasses. He sat next to me on the verandah in the cool night air, his arm spread along the back of my chair as if to envelope me in his embrace.

"I feel it's only fair I warn you that I intend to spend the entire weekend with you and I have every intention of sharing your bed."

"Pretty sure of yourself, aren't you?"

"You don't remember me. Why should you? You came to the children's ward at the hospital where I was. Bernie the Bear. You went round every bed and every cot cheering up the kids. You had a smile and a joke for everyone. When you came to me, I could see you had tears in the corners of your eyes but still you were smiling. You asked me what I wanted to be when I grew up. At that stage the doctors didn't know if I was going to get a chance to grow up. But I said, 'I want to be just like you.' You told me being an actor was a hard business and that I needed to go to acting school. You mentioned a few of the best and told me that if I really, really wanted it then it would happen. You gave me something to strive for.

"I didn't just think about how miserable and how sick I was all the time, from that moment on I had a dream. It was that dream that kept me going. You, Bernie Everson, are the light of my life."

I was decidedly uncomfortable now. I didn't want someone to seduce me because they felt grateful. Pierce saw my discomfort.

"Don't overanalyze, Bernie. This is not a gratitude fuck. I fancy you. You're one hot dude."

I pooh poohed that idea pretty quick smart.

"You're one hot bear, Bernie. I love bears, which is why I made myself over in your image. I'm just a cub at present but give me time."

"What is it you want, Pierce?"

"Isn't it obvious?"

"Not to me."

He began to unbutton my shirt, revealing my pelt as his fingers worked lower and lower. His knuckles grazed my nipples which were so hard they formed little fleshy stalagmites on my chest. He pinched them between his thumb and forefinger sending an electrical impulse straight to my balls. He chewed each in turn, sucking and gnawing until they were tender. He unbuckled my belt, lowering the zip fly on my jeans so he could pull my shirt out. Peeling it off my shoulders and down my arms, he ran his fingers through my thick fur humming his pleasure.

I ran my fingers through his hair as he licked my chest before kissing his way down across my belly. My skin was alive, everywhere Pierce touched me sent a spark to my groin like I had never felt before. He pushed my jeans down and I lifted so he could skin them over my ass. I kicked them off so all I had on were my undies, my cock tenting the material to draw attention to its needs.

"Beautiful," he said as he sucked me through the thin fabric, the pre-cum making stains which he sucked reverently.

He looked up into my eyes as he yanked my briefs off. "Tell me you love to have someone eat that furry ass of yours."

"Beg me, boy, and my ass is yours."

"Please, sir, let me get my tongue in your ass."

"Start on my balls, cub, and work your way round."

Pierce kneeled between my legs, licking my ball sack and sucking each of my heavy plums into his mouth, savoring my musky masculinity. He ran his nose up the shaft of my cock before his tongue darted out to taste the pearl that had formed in the slit.

He did no more than that although I knew we both wanted to take it further. He had other things on his mind for now and I pulled my knees back against my chest to give him access to my hot furry hole. He pulled my cheeks apart, lapping up and down the crack, across the puckered opening, almost as if he were circling his target. Then I felt the tell-tale push of his tongue against my entrance. I love it when a guy eats my ass, matting the hair with his saliva. I pushed my ass lips open so he could get his tongue farther up inside me, giving him the hint that I was ready for him.

He slicked me up until I felt my ass was wet enough to take him. "Fuck me, cub. Fuck Daddy Bear."

"I've wanted to do this for so long," he panted, hurrying to strip off his clothes. When he was finally naked he spat in his hand, massaging it into his cock. It was a magnificent piece of meat. Not too big, not too small, but just right. I knew later in the weekend, I would get an opportunity to taste it, just as I would have an opportunity to bury my nose, my tongue, as well as my cock in Pierce's hot hole.

I felt the head of his prick push against my wet entrance, the flash of pain forcing me to gasp for breath.

"Did I hurt you, Daddy Bear?"

"Nothing to complain of. Fuck me. Fuck me hard."

He slid his cock all the way into my anal chute as I tightened my muscles against the invasion, which just made it more pleasurable for him.

"You are so beautiful," he whispered, pressing his lips to mine.

As he began to piston in and out of my ass he licked my face, mashing his light beard against my darker, bushier one. I ran my fingers down his back, feeling the hair catch in my fingers. My cub would be a bear to reckon with one day soon.

Shit, I was already thinking of him as 'my cub.' Much too early for that.

Instead of thinking too much I concentrated on the full feeling in my ass as he fucked me with increasing speed, forcing the breath out of me as his belly rubbed against mine, engorging my prick until it wanted to explode.

He whispered sweet words of love in my ear as he pounded me into submission. Our relationship was going to be a constant fight for supremacy. For tonight, I'd let him win.

"I can't hold off any longer," he wheezed.

"Come for me, baby. Fill my ass with your bear cream."

As he flooded my guts with his spunk, my own cock, rubbed once too many times, squirted its pent-up load onto my belly and chest, matting our hair as Pierce leaned on me for support as the last shots of his cum squirted deep inside me.

We lay like that for a considerable time, caressing each other, running our fingers over each other's bodies in an early effort at exploration.

Pierce's cock plopped out of my ass with the sound of a small moist fart.

"That was just for starters," he boasted as I felt his cum dribble out of me. "There's a lot more where that came from." He looked in my eyes. "You know this is for keeps, don't you?"

I nodded, too emotional to trust my voice.

He stood, scooping me up into his arms.

"We are gonna spend the entire weekend fucking our brains out, until our balls shrivel up from too much use. On Monday we're gonna go get your old job back so you and I can be on television together like it was meant to be. Right?"

"Right," I agreed.

Then he carried me across the threshold, my ass leaking drops of spunk onto the polished wooden floor like a trail of wet confetti.

# BUSTING A GUT

It was the first cock Con had ever tasted apart from his boyfriend's. It tasted slightly salty, and the foreskin, the first he'd seen up close and personal, smelled of soap and piss, while the texture was like damp human seaweed in his mouth. He didn't stop to ask himself what he thought it would be like because, well, he had never expected to be in this situation.

He believed in love and fidelity and all those other impossible dreams that the movies and television peddled, although it was getting harder to hold on to them. He'd been young and naïve when he met Reg and was quickly seduced into a relationship. At first, it had gone well and Con was in a constant state of euphoria, just as Reg's constant priapic state meant there was a bountiful supply of sex, something Con discovered he liked. A lot.

In fact, Con liked everything about the physical side of romance: the touching, the kissing, the cuddling, and the fucking. Reg, however, had stopped kissing him after they'd moved in together. Everything except Con giving up his ass had stopped once he'd moved his life into Reg's apartment. It was like he was owned by his boyfriend now. He knew it wasn't supposed to be like that.

Now, he was more used to his boyfriend's boozy prick being wedged brutally and angularly down his throat. The one thing Reg didn't thrust down his throat was his tongue. Con missed that most in his relationship – a relationship that was stale as the piss his husband spattered on the floor around the toilet bowl with his near misses after a night out with the boys.

He didn't have time to think about Reg as all his senses were abuzz with the new experience he was storing up to luxuriate over later. Was he enjoying it? That he couldn't really tell. The newness colored all. It had nothing to do with the morality. That he would assuage by lighting a candle; the burnt-out stubs on the altar hard and inflexible like his lover's prick.

No, he was savoring, rather than enjoying. Enjoyment would come with experience. He realized what that thought encompassed: he was already thinking he would do it again. Yes, he would have to get used to the taste of Mark's cock but, after all, he had got used to Reg's sperm though, as often as not, he spat it surreptitiously into a handkerchief he kept beside the bed.

Mark had already sucked him off – and swallowed – and this was Con's reciprocation. That was a new concept for him. Sex meant Reg blew his load in Con's mouth or his ass before turning over and farting his contentment, if not his contempt. He had never come while Reg was inside him. In fact, on the odd occasion Con had begun to jerk his own neglected cock while Reg was nailing him to the bed, his boyfriend had told him to 'quit it' as it was throwing him off his rhythm. Con had only ever had sex with two people in his entire middle-aged life. The comparison was odious.

As he probed his tongue under Mark's foreskin, learning new skills to please an unfamiliar lover, attempting to imitate all that had been done to him a mere half hour before, he realized how clumsy he was, how inexperienced. He knew Mark would not complain, unlike Reg who had expected Con to have the skills of a whore even though he'd been a virgin on their first night together.

He smiled that it was Reg, indirectly, who had led him to Mark. It was after another of their blazing rows; well, actually, Reg's blazing row because Con never raised his voice. He usually cowered against the onslaught, sending his mind wandering away from the cruelty of his boyfriend's tongue, until Reg eventually screamed himself hoarse and slumped drunkenly in front of the TV, drooling over his tank top.

Con needed to escape the foul atmosphere that pervaded their home, poisoning everything in it. He'd taken to wandering the streets of their neighborhood until he'd discovered the small oasis of a park named after some long dead and long forgotten bureaucrat or sportsman. It had a rusting children's play area at one end, a meandering brick paved walking path through stunted native bushes, and an old brick dunny which was permanently locked. The benches had wooden slats missing. Con didn't mind, he loved his little park. It felt as neglected as he did. The park brought him peace, if not tranquility.

It was on one such excursion to what he had come to think of as 'his park' because it was always deserted, he first saw Mark, not that he knew his name at that stage. Admittedly, Con was a little later than usual because Reg had come home after overtime and launched into a bitter attack from which Con had fled after feeding his man. Mark was one of a flurry, yes that was the word that had popped up in his head as he watched them, a flurry of men who were boisterously circumnavigating the park.

He'd envied the camaraderie of the half dozen men aged between, he guessed 25 and 50. They glanced at him the first time they passed by. On the second they smiled at him. The third time he smiled back. By the fifth they asked him to join them. Envying their bond and chatter, he had joined them shyly. He was not as fit as the others and had difficulty keeping up. He discovered they were a group of friends to whom the gym was anathema – too much like hard work – and this was their attempt to remain physically active after a day at their sedentary desk jobs.

It fell to Mark to partner him. Mark was dark and masculine and aged around 35, Con guessed. They had little in common. Mark had an active social life which sounded all-too-blatant to Con's taste.

"Aren't you worried about repercussions?" Con asked. "Especially at work?"

Reg had warned him about being 'obvious.' He hated those 'fag radicals' who had to rub people's noses in their sexual activity. Any time a so-called 'spokesperson' was interviewed on television, Reg went into a paroxysm of rage, screaming 'That faggot doesn't speak for us,' even though Con often thought what the person said made a lot of sense. Con wondered what Reg would think now that he was talking to 'one of them.'

Mark laughed, but not in a malicious way. "No, my boss is gay. The company is gay owned. Besides, I'm good at my job, very good. If an employer can't accept me as I am, then 'fuck off!' I'm not changing for anyone."

Con thought Mark's thinking was just so subversive, he might be just a little bit dangerous. Failing to recognize that his opinions were more Reg's than his own independent thought, Con quickly made an excuse to escape. He knew Mark did not believe his reasons for running off, but that was no matter, he would never see him again. It's not that Mark or any of the other men had put any sort of indecent proposition to him. They'd all been friendly and he'd enjoyed having someone to talk to. No, someone who actually listened to what he said. However, he was glad now he had been wily, and given away little about himself. His church-loving family had warned him of those 'perverts who demand more and more so-called rights in an attempt to foist their unnatural lifestyle on God-fearing Christians.' Even Reg agreed they were always sprouting off about something or the other that just drew attention to themselves, causing more problems than it was worth. Nothing good would come of it. Con had jumped from the proverbial frying pan.

Mark called out to his retreating back, "We're here Mondays, Wednesdays and Thursdays if you'd like to join us again."

"There's no joining fee," another man had called.

Con blushed with embarrassment but later, his boyfriend lying beside him, snoring, he remembered how it felt to be part of a group no matter how peripherally. Over the next few weeks he tried to go back but... He didn't understand what it was that halted his steps a block away. He'd watched the group from his vantage point down the street on a number of occasions. But his feet would not move any farther, no matter how much his heart longed for it.

Until the evening, that is, he'd been grasped firmly by the arm and escorted down the street to the park by Mark who had come up behind him. He allowed himself to be led as he knew he'd never make it on his own. The other men greeted him warmly as if it had been only yesterday that they'd last seen him.

"Ready to get in some exercise?" Mark asked. It was a friendly enquiry unlike the aggressive criticism of his husband who would smack his belly during sex and say, "Your big fat hairy gut is disgusting!" His boyfriend was always on at him to diet and get laser treatment for the hair that sprouted all over his body. Reg claimed fucking his hairy ass was like sticking his dick in a fur rug.

When Con had reluctantly removed his shirt for the first time because he simply couldn't stand the heat any more as the group moved around the park, he closed his eyes in expectation of catcalls and criticism. He was wearing a tank top but the hair that sprouted like weeds all over his chest and back, could not be disguised. To Con's surprise, Mark licked his lips and mumbled, "Yum. A bear."

He asked one of the other men in the group what Mark meant by 'bear,' surprised to discover it was a compliment. It made Con look at Mark in an entirely different light. He supposed his walking companion was around the same age as himself, although his body was firm and fit, not flabby like his own. He allowed that Mark was what people would call 'good-looking,' and he had an open and friendly personality. Con made the comparison but immediately deleted it from his memory. Mark was the antithesis of Reg.

Over the following weeks Con grew to enjoy these three-times-a-week fitness exercises, his confidence increasing along with his energy levels. He wasn't losing any weight to speak of, but he found he didn't get as puffed walking to the shops or to the station. He kept Reg in the dark about his activities, merely intimating he was trying to get rid of the fat accumulated over the years in which the two of them had led an insular existence without friends, without a social life…without hope. Reg suggested facetiously that Con was seeing someone on the side, although he made it perfectly clear what the end result of that would be – for Con. "You'd need extensive dental work and a long stretch in hospital if I ever catch you playing around with anyone else," he threatened. Then, as if the mere idea of Con cheating was ludicrous, he added, "Nah, not possible. Who'd want an ugly, fat, hairy scrubber like you?"

Con was inured to his taunts.

The men in the exercise group usually asked him to join them for coffee at a local café but he declined because he knew Reg would be angry. He didn't like him wasting money on luxuries, and coffee at a café was a luxury as it was something he could easily make at home.

More and more reluctantly, Con said goodbye to the group before heading back to the apartment. The work-out invigorated him. Made him feel good. Leaving the friendly group to return to Reg made him feel the opposite.

It was the night Reg called to say he'd be late as he was working overtime. Con knew better. He saw his pay slips. He was careless. There was never any overtime listed. He knew he had extra-curricular sexual activity. He didn't care. It lightened Con's load because Reg always came home so tired he left him alone and went straight to sleep. If anything, Con felt sorry for the other man, or men. Con had a little of his own money; he didn't dare touch Reg's stash at the back of his sock drawer, as his boyfriend counted it assiduously.

If it was good enough for Reg to lie, it was surely okay for Con to join his new friends for a latte and a light snack. At the coffee shop, he opened up more than ever and told them about Reg. Just enough to elicit sympathy, not enough to paint him the total bastard that he was. It was a wrench when it came time to leave, but he still had time to get home before Reg returned from his 'overtime.' Or so he thought.

Something was wrong. The lights were ablaze when he walked through the front gate of their modest Federation cottage. Not just the lamp he left on to convince burglars someone was home; all the lights were blazing. As he put his key in the lock the front door was wrenched open.

"He's drunk," Con thought. "Something's gone wrong with his 'overtime'."

Reg ranted at him about his dinner, his dereliction of domestic duties; called him as many names as he could lay an expletive to, but Con took it all with equanimity. He did not answer back, he merely went about his so-called duties and made Reg his meal which only succeeded in making him more furious. Later, when Con declined his fumbled lovemaking, Reg threw him on the bed, and backhanded him enough to split his lip. Reg pummeled his ass with his prick, and thumped his body with his fists, but Con would not give him the satisfaction of breaking. He went inside himself to spend time with the friends who treated him as a person, not as a domestic slave or a number of orifices to fuck at will.

Two days later the group was so appalled at Con's state, they threatened to call the police, social services, the men's refuge: all to no avail. Con merely smiled, telling them he would take care of it. That was the first time he went home with Mark. The first time someone made love to him. It was such a revelation, he suspected he had no idea what love was all about. But he was willing to learn.

Reg beat him when he arrived home late, demanding to know where he'd been.

"With friends," Con told him simply, and no amount of cross examination or shouting got more out of him.

Con had finally had enough. He knew he could never leave Reg because the bastard would track him down and make his life a misery, and he didn't want to involve any of the others in his problems. He'd think on it awhile.

Over the weeks that followed, Con confided to his friendlier neighbors who showed concern at his battered state, that he believed Reg was having an affair. He cried that he was terrified Reg was going to leave him. Those taken into his confidence commiserated publicly while clucking privately that it would be the best thing that ever happened.

It was a Friday. Con was preparing fish for Reg's dinner. Regardless of his personal hygiene or his sexual habits, Reg was a spiritual fundamentalist. Con was tired of filleting and cooking his fish. He'd tried once to buy fish and chips from the local shop but Reg had thrown the hot fatty meal in his face, burning him. Reg wanted it like his mother used to make, so Con bought fresh fish weekly from the market, taking it home to scale and clean.

Con was slicing the fish open to rip out its guts, flinging them into the old-fashioned sink disposal when the doorbell rang. He knew Reg would make no effort to answer. Wiping his bloodied hands on his apron, he realized half-way to the front door that he still had the fish knife in his hands.

Con smiled broadly when he opened the door. The man was blond and handsome, dressed totally unlike the usual dark and handsome Mark. He was wearing a tight-fitting vulgar T-shirt with the scrawled slogan, Take Me, I'm Yours, plus a pair of jeans that were so tight he must have poured himself into them and which showed off his bubble butt to perfection.

"Come in," Con said ushering the guy into the living room. Reg's eyes lit up when he saw him. "Well, hello," he said, conspicuously rearranging his crotch. "Who's this then?"

"You must be Reg?" the visitor said.

Reg was leering. "You a friend of Con's? Pity I never met you before. But there's no time like the present to catch up."

"I'm a very special friend of Con's."

"Maybe you'd like to be my special friend, too?" Reg grabbed a handful of his crotch to highlight its availability.

"No," he said. "Con has all I need."

The blond man grabbed Con and kissed him, running his hands fondly across his body.

Reg was shocked at the blatant disregard for his proprietorial interests. Initially. Then he thought he saw potential.

"Don't get me wrong, I'm not jealous. In fact, this could add that bit of spice missing from our love life."

Reg stood up as Con and the new man fondled each other, quickly stripping off his shirt. His pants and underwear followed until he was totally naked waving his semi-hard prick as if it were somehow inviting. Reg was still smiling as the blood gushed from his groin. Con had been so quick he did not see the fish knife sever his cock and balls. He had even less time as Con struck again, gutting Reg's belly wide open so part of his entrails spilled out. He had just time to register as he fell to the floor, that the visitor was not a natural blond.

Wiping the blade on his apron, Con gave silent thanks that Reg was such a cheap bastard he'd never had the living room carpeted. It was floored with cheap linoleum.

Later, they'd washed Reg's body, dressing it in his best clothes. Con then retrieved the suitcase he'd already packed for him. With Mark holding Reg's body upright with one arm, carrying the suitcase in the other, Con opened the door to let them pass.

"You drunken bastard," Con screamed loudly enough to alert the neighbors. "I give you the best years of my life and this is how you thank me. Well take your stinking blond toy boy and piss off. See what I care. I can look after myself. I don't need you. As for you, you bitch …"

Con threw a vase large enough to make the impact when it hit the pavement theatrical enough to entertain the neighbors who would be peering from behind their blinds, but wide enough of the target that it didn't hit Mark in his impenetrable disguise.

"And don't think I'll ever take you back when this whore kicks your sorry ass out! You walk out now, then don't ever come back. You hear! You hear me!"

He timed it so his shouts would reach a fever pitch as the car drove away. Then he slumped on the front door step sobbing.

When he thought the voyeurs had got enough theatrics for the night he picked himself up, giving one last plaintiff sob before he went inside, closing the door quietly on his performance.

It would take some time before Mark would dispose of the body in a spot where no one would ever find it, and then he would take the hire car back, leaving it outside the showroom before ditching his disguise.

Con hummed softly; it wouldn't do for the neighbors to hear him, and went into the kitchen. He turned on the sink disposal and fed him boyfriend's penis into the mechanism.

# STEAM PUNK

There were signs everywhere for Wankers, Circle Jerks, and Carpet Munchers. I felt like I was in some sleazy sauna or rave party instead of at an inner city pub where it looked as if you could forfeit your life or pick up some sexually transmitted disease, just by going inside. I had no virginity to offer up being a bored hairy 36-year-old bus driver putting on a bit, okay more than a bit, of excess weight because of my sedentary job sitting behind the wheel all day.

I had intended sitting in front of the telly with a beer and a takeaway pizza until late that night before I'd head out on the prowl. The advantage of living in a gay neighborhood was that gay men seemed inordinately reluctant to lower their blinds. That was a godsend for me.

Then *he* came along. He being one of The Wankers. Yep, that's right, a band. It was Neo-Punk night, the torn canvas sign flapping in the breeze proclaimed as much, as did the worn and torn second-hand clothing of the crowd lounging about the entrance of the Duke of Clarence Hotel. Knowing what sort of crowd it would be, I'd done my best to camouflage my age, my weight, and my natural musical inclinations, although I knew I'd never assimilate with this mob. The best I could hope for was an uneasy truce. After all, I could be someone's supportive uncle or older brother or, even better, a record producer scouting new talent for his independent label.

I didn't even know *his* name. I was driving the bus he'd hopped on at one of the busy suburban stops. Jet black hair hung over one eye, his skin as pasty white as kindergarten potato glue, he sported the obligatory piercings to eyebrows, lips, ears, and nose. I could see more, outlined through his black T-shirt, around his nipples. I also suspected he had piercings in much more intimate places. In all, he was carrying enough metal to build a small patrol boat.

As soon as he opened his mouth to speak there was the tell-tale sparkle of a stud through his tongue. I got hard. There was something about this kid. I judged he was in his early twenties: that sure warmed my balls. But he was short forty-five cents for his fare.

"Aw, dude, I didn't know the fares went up today. This is all the money I got," he moaned. "Please, man, I gotta get to rehearsal. We're playing an important gig tonight." He brandished his guitar as if that were proof of what he was saying.

"Are you any good?" I smiled.

"We suck, man. We play like shit," and he smiled back.

"If you don't got the fare, get off the bus," a passenger yelled.

"Come on, driver, get this bus moving. I have appointments to get to," some anonymous person called from the back. There was a general murmur of irritation.

He glared at the passengers, some of whom pretended they had no interest in our little tête-a-tête although others glared back belligerently or busied themselves in their books and their newspapers. I knew if I let him on the bus at least one of them would be on to my supervisor complaining about 'human trash' being allowed to ride for free. Reaching into my pocket I dragged out some cash and gave it to him. I made a show of it because I wanted the cheap uncharitable fuckers to see it, more to protect myself than from any expectation of public gratitude.

He handed his fare over and I duly gave him a ticket. And change. That way he'd have enough for the fare back, at least. He whistled loudly and tunelessly, his 'fuck-you' gesture to the other passengers as he made his way down the aisle to the back of the vehicle. I had to chuckle. It was a very small highlight in my otherwise pitifully dull life. I adjusted my uncomfortably hard cock and steered the bus out into the traffic.

I watched him in my passenger mirror on the long ride into the city. He sat on his own, the other passengers obviously scared of his look, and he oblivious to his surroundings as he closed his eyes to practice his songs for the gig on air guitar, silently mouthing the lyrics.

He was a good-looking fucker and I had a hard time concentrating.

Once the bus reached the run-down industrial suburbs skirting of the central business district, I noticed he got his gear together to alight in a once working-class suburb that had been slowly taken over by squatters and uni students, the area now noted for its thriving music pubs and artistic scene.

After pressing the bell, he made his way down the bus and stood next to me as I pulled into the stop.

"Thanks mate. I owe ya. Not many people would have done what you did," he said.

"Glad to help. You don't owe me anything. Good luck with the gig tonight."

Thrusting a flyer at me, he got off the bus almost as if he were embarrassed. I waved to him as I pulled away from the kerb. He started to raise his hand then obviously thought better of it. Probably didn't suit his punk/emo/Goth image to wave. I wasn't sure which of the subcultures he was. Not that it mattered. They all got a bad rap. Unjustified, in my opinion. Not that anyone was asking.

That's how I came to find myself seated at the bar among a crowd of youngsters around half my age listening to a group of salaciously named neo-punk bands whose loudness far outstripped their musical ability, although that in no way detracted from the enjoyment. There were lots of lyrics about 'fucking the system,' 'fucking the Man,' as well as fucking in general. Most of the audience gave me as wide a berth as my bus passengers gave the punk musician, probably confused as to whether I was a cop or a pervert. I guess I just didn't have the charisma for a record company exec.

The Wankers were headliners, so they were on last. The pub was overflowing onto the surrounding streets by the time the obviously popular band was announced, the venue audience breaking out into loud whoops and applause. At least I found out my punk boy's name. Seems he had only one: Steam. Appropriate really as he was as pale as steam and as wispy in personality. It was an assumed moniker like those of the other band members who were known as Johnny Granite, Pete Snowball, Bad Attitude, and the drummer was Casey Thrum. The names were the most original thing about them.

Maybe I was biased but it seemed to me that Steam, singer and guitarist, was clearly way out in front of the other talent from earlier in the night, and a cut above the other members of his own band. The crowd in the pub quieted down, people moving closer to the makeshift stage, some young chicks even flashing their tits as he strode to the microphone.

Surveying the audience as he adjusted the mike, he saw me perched at the bar and unselfconsciously nodded his recognition. I held my beer up in salute, a hundred eyes turning in my direction. That one acknowledgement from Steam was enough for a distinct change in attitude on the part of the audience. A few guys even brought me a drink on the strength of it.

The band was rough and unpolished, as were their songs penned by Steam and Johnny, but they had an excitement that was missing from the other groups that night. I guess I shouldn't have been jealous of the girls who flirted outrageously with my gorgeous punk God, it wasn't like the kid was gay, and even if he were, he wasn't likely to be interested in an overweight hairy bear my age.

Still, I liked him. I couldn't take my eyes off him, from his first number screamed with a rage I was too old and numb to feel, through songs about 'taking a chance' and 'living for the moment,' to the final paroxysm of pain and longing in "Angel in the Mist." The audience erupted as the final wail of Steam's voice echoed around the neighborhood. I stood to applaud and whistle. If he wasn't signed up soon to a record deal, there was no justice.

I didn't have much of a chance to thank him for taking me out of my comfort zone, for something so special I would never forget it, because he was swamped as he jumped down off the stage, leaving his guitar for one of the band to take back to the dressing room. He was waylaid by a number of young women who wanted him to autograph their tits as they thrust what was obviously their phone number into his jeans pocket. He kept his eye on me as he played the crowd going so far as to nibble a nipple or two, squeeze a breast and even give one or two of the lucky girls a quick pash. God, it made me wish I was a teenage girl with big tits.  Was it too late for gender realignment?

When he finally reached me he still had a number of the audience vying for his attention.

"You were great," I said. I kicked myself that I sounded so feeble.

"Thanks. I tried to make it extra special tonight."

I was about to ask him why, but people were yanking on his arms.

"Look," he said. "I can't talk now, how about you drop in and see my next performance. You might like it even more. Wednesday night, around midnight. If you stay up that late, old man." He winked to show he was jesting. "We can talk then."

He thrust a flyer into my jeans; this was getting to be a habit. His hand brushed my obvious hard-on and for an instant his gaze met and held mine, but he was jostled away before he could comment, although he called,

"Please come. Live dangerously," as he disappeared in the melee.

Finishing my beer, I adjusted my erection and headed home; not at all sorry I'd made the effort to check out his talent. Straight, bi, or gay, he was an immensely likeable young man beneath the metal and the brooding personality. I could have watched him for hours.

I was preoccupied with driving for the next few days, having given no thought to Steam's invitation. While it was flattering to my ego, did I have enough in common with the punk lad to make any sort of friendship viable? I didn't think so. Maybe he was after money. Nah, he must know bus drivers are not exactly top of the food chain, although I obviously had more ready cash than he did. Besides, I wasn't sure how much of his sort of music I could take before it did my head in. Once was fine, but…

It was late Wednesday evening before I gave him another thought, and then mainly because of a dud hook-up via the net. The guy looked hot in his photograph, swearing it had been taken within the past twelve months. He was pleasant on the eye, with a good body, although not so good to put him out of my league (like Steam, my brain inserted into my thoughts unbidden), and available. Alas, the guy who turned up at my door had really let himself go if that was a true photo on his stats page. Look, I'm not finicky, but this guy was grossly overweight, wearing an obvious toupee and was a good twenty years older than the photo. I couldn't even bring myself to go through with it just for the sake of not having to go out looking for another pick-up. I let him down as gently as possible, something he seemed to expect, closed the door and went in search of the jeans I was wearing when Steam slipped the leaflet in my pocket.

I found them in the linen basket ready for the wash, the flyer still where he'd put it. I laughed out loud when I turned it over. The fucker wasn't performing with his band, he was flying solo at *Steam'n'Hot*, one of the city's popular gay sex-on-premises saunas, noted for its incredibly steamy, but highly illegal, strip shows. Of course, Steam was probably just stripping for a few bucks; it didn't mean he was gay. In fact, it usually meant the opposite.

The shows were rarely advertised except by word-of-mouth and the strippers were seldom the same. They were usually would-be male models or out-of-work actors, down on their luck, eager to make ends meet. The sauna crowd liked its strippers butch and dangerous. You could make good money, so the rumor had it, if you displayed wood; even better money if you left a shiny deposit on the stage after your act. That's where the illegal came in.

As I said, it was all rumor because I'd never been on the receiving end of word-of-mouth. Besides, with my hairy body and beer gut, I wasn't exactly what guys who go to saunas look for. I guess I didn't have to cruise the sauna after the show, but I was wise enough to know that seeing the underside of Steam's talent would get me horny as fuck. I'd need to get my rocks off once I'd seen him naked. God, I was so predictable. That, however, was not enough to stop me from heading out on my 'Date with Destiny,' to appropriate another of Steam's song titles.

My name wasn't at the door when I arrived, so I had to pay admission. I'd missed the early show, but didn't begrudge the payment. I got my towel and a locker key, feeling a bit out of place as I headed to the change area where a quick glance at some of the ageing bodies assuaged my embarrassment a little. Once stripped I wound the towel around my waist, and regretted all those extra portions I'd snuck onto my plate over the years when I had no one to look my best for. I placed the key around my neck, looking at myself in the mirror. There were a couple of good years left in the old body yet.

I tried watching TV in the bar and juice area, but I couldn't hear the sound over an old queen who was telling his acolytes about the stud who'd just fucked him into the floor. It sounded more wishful thinking than reality, quite sad really. The sauna was standing room only, but that was because those on their feet were being taken care of orally by those seated on the wooden benches. Nether position appealed at the moment. Ditto the orgy room, the sling room, the water sports room, or the Jacuzzi.

A PA announcement made choosing moot. "Gentlemen, and I use that term advisedly, the show you've all been waiting for will commence in the bar area in ten minutes. Those wishing to attend should make their way to the bar area now."

There seemed an inordinate amount of haste among the denizens of the sauna. I joined them in their exodus, grabbing one of the last bar stools available, the area in front of me packed to capacity very quickly. The crowd was buzzing with anticipation.

"What's the attraction?" I asked an elderly chap seated beside me.

"This kid is the hottest thing since rhubarb flavored condoms," he said as if that explained all.

My quizzical look spurred him on. "Punk kid. Tattoos, piercings, wild hair, typical mugger-in-a-dark alley look. Pale as a vampire, slim body but with muscles like marble. Can make you come just by looking at you."

That was the best description of Steam I'd ever heard.

As the lights dimmed, a blanket of fog belched out to cover the small stage area. Then with a scream I was familiar with from attending The Wankers' concert, the doleful pulsing beat of "Angel in the Mist" blasted through the bar area. I smiled at the narcissism involved in stripping to the soundtrack of his own voice.

I didn't smile long as a spot picked out Steam striding triumphantly from back stage. He was confident, he was aggressive, and he looked so powerful I almost shot off in my towel.

"I see what you mean," I whispered to my companion.

"You ain't seen nothing yet."

There was no way Steam could see me where I was at the back of the audience in the semi-light. He would think I hadn't shown up.

He mimed his own lyrics as he strode the stage like he owned the premises, discarding each item of clothing with disdain, like he was doing us all a favor. I felt like a pervert watching him, especially as my cock was rock hard. After each article of clothing he strummed his air guitar, bumping his body in a wanton display of arousal. It wasn't the audience turning him on, it was his own voice coming out of the cheap sound system. Steam was the ultimate narcissist, admiring his own beauty, reflected in the mirrors all around the venue, rubbing his hands sensually across his chest and stomach.

Finally, all he had between him and the way he was born was a pair of very skimpy briefs that showed the outline of a very substantial cock. He ran his fingers along the stiff outline seductively before turning his back to the audience. From what I could see, his ass was firm and round. He peeked over his shoulder at the audience, his finger playing coyly with his bottom lip. He looked, simultaneously, innocent as a schoolboy and the personification of lasciviousness. He lowered his briefs down over his muscular cheeks, parting his legs before bending forward to give the audience a glimpse of his snug inviting hole. If I wasn't mistaken, there was the tell-tale glint of a dried sperm trail down his crack. Plus his ass hole was dilated. That gave me more than enough detail to store as fantasy to beat off over for weeks to come.

I had a thing for twinks, but so few of them were into hairy, beer-bellied bus drivers who wanted them to…let's not go there. It makes me sound like a predator.

Steam was stringy but muscular, bars through both tits and, my guess was right, piercings around his cock and balls. He was inked in stripes down one side of his torso which made him look even hotter to me. He slid his briefs down over his thick bovver boy boots and white socks, kicking them into the audience. There was a flurry of pushing and shoving as three or four men fought for the treasure. The ultimate winner went back to his seat grinning broadly, placing the briefs to his nose and sniffing theatrically.

Steam jumped down from the makeshift stage, gyrating to the music, allowing members of the audience to run their hands across his body, pinching his nipples, fingering his butt hole, squeezing his nuts or his oozing prick. Then they would lean down and stuff cash in his socks before he moved on to the next punter.

He gave each patron around the same amount of attention, perhaps slightly favoring those who gave more generously, although he never obviously looked at the cash in his socks. Somehow, he seemed to sense the magnanimity of his benefactors. As he approached, my companion extracted a few bank notes from his pocket and I thought it would be wise of me to do the same.

Steam sidled up to the guy on the stool next to me, never once breaking eye contact with him, devoting his entire attention to the stranger who groaned as he squeezed Steam's generous prick before fingering his butt. The guy juddered a few times, as he obviously shot his load into his towel. Steam caressed the side of his face before turning his attention to me. At first he looked startled, then he smiled and whispered, "So you turned up, old man?"

"How could I resist?"

"I missed you at the first show. I thought you weren't coming."

Steam straddled me, riding the ridge of my stiff cock hidden under my towel. "Mmm," he sighed.

"If you keep that up, you will have me coming," I said, leaning over to put twenty bucks with all the other cash. I noticed a few fifties and one or two hundred-dollar notes. My offering seemed pretty lame in comparison.

He planted his lips against mine, burrowing his tongue between my teeth until he was exploring my mouth. He tasted of peppermint and…spunk. I pulled back involuntarily. Steam cupped his hand over his mouth to smell his breath.

"Sorry," he blushed. "I thought the peppermint would hide it."

"And what am I likely to find here?" I said, pushing my thumb against his butthole.

"Peppermint stings," he laughed.

My thumb sank into his warm anal canal without much resistance. I pulled out and sucked my thumb, savoring ball juice.

"You have been busy."

"I guess I should have warned you, eh?"

I shrugged. "You don't owe me any explanations."

"I'm not giving you any. I think my behavior is pretty self-explanatory. But I should have prepared you for it."

"Maybe," I said. "Yeah, definitely."

"Sorry."

"Are you sorry because you sucked somebody off earlier or sorry because your attempt to disguise it failed?"

"I'm sorry if I've upset you," he said.

"Why?"

"I like you." To prove his point he rubbed his hands across my furry belly and up to my chest.

"Because I paid your fare?"

He looked offended. "Hell no! Don't take this the wrong way, I'm grateful and everything, but it was a couple of bucks. When I saw you sitting in the pub watching my performance, I liked you watching me."

"And I liked watching you perform."

"But you thought I could perform for an audience of one."

"That's the usual configuration," I said without rancor.

"Not for everyone."

Before I could ask him any more questions, my time was up and he moved on to the next audience member. I wasn't getting any extra favors.

My companion seemed to know most things about Steam, so I whispered, "Is that his whole act."

"Hell, no," he responded. "Now it gets really interesting. His show earlier was so hot, management asked him to tone it down in case the joint got raided."

"Is this a regular event?

"Unfortunately not. I guess the kid only does it when he's broke. You have to keep your ear open when the gossip advertises Steam Heat night. That's his name, Steam. He has a reputation and a real loyal following. Sometimes he disappears for months at a time. I think he plays in a boy band or something like that."

I didn't correct the guy's misconception, but I knew Steam would be pretty pissed off that someone called The Wankers a boy band.

By this time Steam had completed a circuit of the audience and was back on stage. I marveled that his body wasn't black and blue from the pinching and biting and twisting that members of the audience had perpetrated on him. The music got decidedly heavier when the tracks changed, the music's driving beat throbbing in my hard cock. Steam slouched in a plastic chair that an assistant had placed while Steam did his gyrations around the room.

He pulled his legs up over his shoulders, sliding down in the seat so he could expose his smooth slick asshole. That sly smile played around his lips as he surveyed his admirers, some men quite openly stroking their cocks, before nodding to one of the men, who was immediately high-fived by his mates before stumbling up on stage. The assistant brought out a tub of lube. The chosen one dipped his hand in it before slathering Steam's ass, pushing three fingers into the rubbery sphincter.

Steam writhed against the invading digits, pushing against them like he wanted to be fucked hard. The guy from the audience obliged, drilling him savagely until he had four fingers in Steam's ass.

I turned to my companion whose eyes seemed glazed over with lust. "I take it the kid is gay."

He shook his head sadly, then qualified it. "Only for pay."

"He's a hustler?"

"Uh huh. A few of the wealthy guys who turn up at every gig have offered him the world but he turns them all down. He could live very comfortably if he gave in. And it's not like he has any qualms about doing anything or anyone. He's one young twisted punk." The guy whispered in my ear some of the rumors about what Steam got up to. I'm not surprised he didn't want to say it out loud because it was enough to turn most people's stomachs. "But that sort of thing really costs."

Damn. Now I knew why he'd invited me along tonight. I was just another sucker in a long line of cash transactions. What a disappointment. I preferred my fantasy unsullied. Who was I kidding? This way I got to feel him up if I felt like splurging a little cash. I could make it up with a bit of overtime. Sure, it was galling that I thought he liked me, but life is full of disappointments, isn't it?

A second audience member was now on stage pressing a large rubber dildo into Steam's pliable ass lips

"Hey, Steam," one of the audience shouted. "Where's Lucky tonight?"

"Had to leave him at home. Management won't allow him on the premises."

Some members of the audience laughed loudly.

"What's wrong with Lucky?" I asked my companion.

"German shepherds are not permitted. It's a health hazard."

Before I could enquire further, there was a cheer from the audience. Steam had climbed down off the stage and up onto the lap of a gross troll in the front row who was waving about a handful of bank notes of a high denomination. People were standing to watch as Steam put his feet on the low armrests on the chair in which his wealthy benefactor was seated, wiggling his ass above the fat slug before easing his hole down over the fat oozing prick. There was applause as Steam sank down to the old cunt's balls, a look of absolute pleasure on his face.

I suppose I should have felt sickened by the display, or adopted the moral high ground over the punk musician's indiscriminate paid promiscuity, but the fact of the matter was it was hot watching Steam enjoying himself so licentiously. That he was gay for pay added an extra frisson to the proceedings.

He sucked face with the old goat whose prick was embedded in his ass, bumping up and down to impale himself on that thick pole. He seemed genuinely to enjoy the penetration. Either that or he was a better actor than I gave him credit for. I couldn't control my excitement any longer. Without touching myself, I shot a load into the towel that was barely covering my lap. I shuddered, making mewling sounds that must have been louder than I imagined, because Steam was looking directly at me as I opened my eyes after shuddering one of the most intense orgasms I'd ever experienced.

The grotesque older man bellowed his orgasm for the audience to appreciate which sent a few of them scampering to their wallets to extract any ready cash they could come up with. Again I noticed large denomination notes in serious bundles. Even with overtime, it was more money than I could manage.

Steam pulled his ass off the troll's cock, massaged it theatrically, then used his coy trick of the finger on the lower lip, glancing around the room, flirting with everyone, before he called, "Who's next?"

There was pushing and shoving as men waved wads of cash in his face. Steam made his way among the audience, obviously sharp-eyed enough to calculate who was offering the most cash. He was making a circuit of the room to ensure no one missed out on an opportunity to bid for him. It was best I made a strategic withdrawal before he wiggled his beautiful ass in my direction. I guess I'd been daydreaming longer than I thought because when I got up from the bar stool to escape, Steam was blocking my path as he continued to grind his hips.

"Where are you off to, old man?"

"I think I should go."

He pushed his hand between the folds of my towel to grasp my sticky cock, still hard from watching his slutty behavior. He jerked me a few times until he removed his hand to tongue my spunk from his fist.

All he said was "Don't. I know your secret and I like it."

Flustered by his accusation, I pushed past him – more roughly than I meant – forcing my way through the suffocating crowd. As I stumbled out of the area I heard a cheer go up. Steam had obviously chosen his next victim. In my eagerness to escape, I lost my bearings, having to circumnavigate the premises until I found my way back to where I started. Steam was entertaining a group of horny old men, kneeling on the floor as one face fucked him and another reamed his ass. Yeah, it was still hot to watch, especially as he seemed blithely unconcerned by the line waiting to use his body, or the fact they were not the sorts of sex partners he could pull in the normal course of events. I didn't need to see that. I asked a guest the directions to the changing room, and fled.

I needed to catch my breath; my heart was beating ridiculously fast for such a small amount of exercise. I knew, however, it wasn't physical exertion that was the cause, but rather stress watching my fantasy crash and burn. I was such a stupid, old man. I sat on the damp bench and cradled my head in my hands. The locker room was empty so I could give in to my…despair was too strong a word, disappointment perhaps.

I didn't hear him come into the area. The first I knew of his presence was when he straddled my legs and sat on my lap, facing me.

"Well, now you know. I wish you'd stay," he said, wiggling his ass into my crotch so that my cock ached.

"Whoa, boy. You're a bit rich for my blood." My cock was tenting the towel. God, I was an embarrassment.

Steam parted the folds of my towel to grab hold of

my cock, still hard and aching for him. Shifting slightly, he aimed my prick at his hot ass and impaled his sloppy hole. As I slid into the warm porridge in his guts, I couldn't stop the loud gasp that confirmed what he'd already guessed about me. Still, I wasn't about to pay for it. I pushed him, but he would not budge except to drag his ass lips up and down my shaft as he milked me expertly.

"Relax. Don't fight it," he purred.

"I can't afford you," I wheezed, almost prepared to pay anything he asked for the incredible feelings he aroused in me.

He laughed. "I was right about you. I saw it in your eyes at the pub. I saw it magnified a hundred times over here tonight. I would never take your money. I've searched for so long for a man like you."

It was my turn to laugh.

"Scoff all you want, but please don't leave. I wanted to give you a taste, so you know what you'll get later. I have to get back to the show. There's a reason for everything. If you trust me, I'll explain everything later. When all this is over, I need the sauna to get the toxins flushed out of my body. I'd like it if you could be there. I want to get my tongue in that furry ass of yours." He ran his hands lovingly across the fur pelt on my tummy, humming his appreciation. "I want to feel your cock in my ass again. I want to suck you until your balls are dry. Most of all, I want to see that look in your eye while you watch me."

He tugged my hand and I let him drag me back to the area where he'd been performing before. A cheer went up from the crowd. I sat back at the bar while he strode into the sea of human flesh that was ready to devour his youth, his beauty, his body – for a price.

He must have his reasons. As for me, I was only too glad to have my secret aired. Yes, I loved sloppy fucks. I loved watching the man I liked – the man I could very easily love– being fucked into oblivion by the good, the bad, and the ugly. It got my balls churning, it got my heart thumping like crazy, it got my cock hard as granite. That he wanted to chow down on my hairy ass was an added bonus. These were the barriers to any of my previous relationships working. Hell, I was already thinking relationships. When would I ever learn?

As it happened, I didn't learn my lesson that night. Or the next. In fact, it seemed unlikely I would ever learn my lesson. I simply couldn't believe I'd met my match sexually. My ideal match in every way. Later that evening, the bukkake spunk dribbling from his face and chest, after I'd watched a room full of men pay to love Steam for the duration of an orgasm, we'd gone to the steam room where I'd sat and watched as he gave it away for free, afterwards riding me to the exclusion of all others until I thought he would wear away my prick shaft. He drained my balls as he explained he was raising cash for the band that had an opportunity to play parts of Asia where they were just making a name for themselves via their YouTube clips.

His was the fastest and easiest way of raising the capital quickly. In case I misunderstood, he added, "But I also love it, which makes it quite easy for me. It helps enormously that I love sex; that I'm insatiable. I also love to be watched, not just by everyone, but to have that one special man watching me enjoy myself and me knowing he's enjoying himself as much as I am."

It was the first time I'd ever heard someone verbalize my…um…tastes, predilections, call them what you will. It was incredible that he was young, hot and, it seemed, into me, rather than the usual hideous old trolls that usually sought me out. Perhaps, I was the hideous one, although Steam kept assuring me I was everything he looked for in a 'boyfriend.' Yes, he'd even used the B word. Right after he'd buried his face in my fur-lined anal crack, and supped for so long my butthole was in danger of chafing.

Still, I could not get my head around my luck. At the end of the evening, thoroughly exhausted by the fact each and every one of my 'kinks' had been aired and put into performance, Steam revealed a fantasy sex life that beggared belief, although my cock thickened as he outed himself. He grinned like an idiot as he saw the affect he was having on me with his revelations which encouraged him to greater intimacy. It was easy as we were seated in the sauna in the early hours of the morning, alone at last.

When I left, wrung out like an old dishcloth, but with the most amazing skin tone, I began to have doubts. It was all too good to be true. There had to be a catch. To pay for such an amazing catch as Steam, I was obviously destined to be diagnosed with some hideous terminal illness in the next three weeks. Or I would lose my job. Or…the superstitions ran through my brain until I had to scream for them to stop. They had done the trick, however.

Steam and I had made no set arrangement to meet again although we'd both professed a desire to explore our options together – no pressure. He gave me a list of dates and places The Wankers would be appearing, telling me he would love to see me at one or more of them. That night had been his finale as a stripper, 'for the time being' he added quickly in case a future emergency arose, because he'd more than raised the required cash for the band's Asian excursion.

I could see no happy ending to our burgeoning relationship, and Steam was so much what I'd wanted in a partner all my adult life, it would just make the parting all the more painful. I didn't end up going to any of his gigs so I winced each time the bus I was driving pulled into the stop where I'd first met him, and the stop that had been his destination.

I opened the bus door and passengers alighted and others got on. I turned away to steer the bus into the traffic. A late passenger flung himself aboard as I was about to close the vehicle door.

"Oh. Shit. I left my wallet at home. I don't have money for the fare."

I looked up into the most inviting eyes I'd ever seen. Eyes that shone with expectation. My cock was already hard at the sound of his voice. That would make it difficult to drive.

I laughed. "How far you going, mate?"

"All the way, old man. And I'm looking for a like-minded traveling companion."

"Climb aboard," I said, easing the bus into traffic. "We'll work something out."

# PISS ELEGANT

It's no fun walking around snooty Dover Heights in leather harness, leather jeans and biker boots at the best of times. It's even less fun when it's the coldest night of the year and the thick pelt of hair covering your body can't keep you warm. When you're lost and the only people to approach for directions are a gaggle of highly lavender-coiffed matrons with sun-bleached skin the toughness of your accessories, walking their poodles which growl at you as if the leather you're wearing is their long lost relative.

And it's least fun when you know you're running twenty minutes late for a hot date with a new daddy bear master who must, by this time, be extremely pissed off.

**DUNGEON MASTER (Eastern suburbs):** Daddy master seeks cub and otter slaves with eager and insatiable mouths for froth fest and forced feeding. No stamina, then don't reply.

It was as brief as it was belligerent. Almost defiant in its cockiness. It, the personal classified, had caught my eye on one of the dating websites – I call it dating, but it was more like quickblowandgo.com – and I'd responded promptly and subserviently, stressing my unlimited capacity for humiliation and, in turn, received an impersonal form email giving me explicit instructions on where, when, and how low to grovel.

But here I was eagerly anticipating the prospect of warm (recycled) beer unable to find the address. I suspected I may have been deliberately misled in order to make my punishment more pleasurable for him and all the more painful for me. Eventually, however, I did manage to stumble across the block of apartments, the well-disguised entrance of which was as inviting as a hemorrhoidal sphincter muscle, but being the good slave I am, I pressed the bell and adopted a submissive position on the spiky door mat emblazoned with the words *Have A Nice Life*, waiting for the inevitable.

I heard the locks being turned, the door opening.

"I've been very bad, master. I'm late. I deserve to be punished, sir," I whimpered, not daring to look up.

"Jesus Christ, can't any of you guys get it right?" he said. Then he shouted up the stair well. "Todd, there's another one of your slaves down here. Can't you give them the correct fuckin' address instead of doing this to me every time?"

"What's this bastard like, Scott?" a voice boomed from above. "Most of 'em have been dogs."

"I'd give this one a seven," was all Scott called.

A seven? How humiliating.

"Okay fucker!" Master Todd yelled from the landing. Crawl up here on your hands and knees. I wanna see that tongue work overtime clearing up the crud off those steps."

This command to someone who wouldn't so much as lift a finger at home to dust a shelf or polish a doorknob?

For this stranger, though, I was willing to perform my dog act slowly up the tiled stairs – they were comparatively clean although the taste of detergent residue does leave a nasty after-taste. I heard Scott, grumbling his displeasure, close the front door to his flat.

After the stairs my lint-coated tongue did its damnedest to polish Todd's knee-length leather boots, and even though I thought they would have passed parade muster at any barracks, he was well displeased. That resulted in the first of my punishments – a few well directed swats across my bare, by this time freezing, back.

Bearing up under the blows, I scrambled my way into his flat, across the parquet floors. Parquet? I thought that went out in the '70s? Maybe it was retro-parquet. Ah well, you can't be too preoccupied with the exegesis of floor paneling when, I suspected, the parquet was not so much a commitment to interior design as a hint that the living-room rather than the bathroom was to be our play pen. Indeed, his combined living/dining area was his 'dungeon.' I sighed, but I'd had worse.

Todd was a pig. As in slob, not a pig in shit. Cascading beer gut, fetid beer breath. But as masters go he had a good line in verbal abuse and corporal, make that corpulent, punishment but when he told me he wanted the "fuckin' parquet floor to gleam like the side of a Qantas Jumbo Jet" I reared on my knees, looked him right in the eye, informing him: "I'm a slave, mate, not a fuckin' cleaner."

For my troubles I got a severe lick of his crop and quickly ducked back on all fours, my tongue resolutely flicking in and out like a pop-eyed gecko. To help keep my throat well-lubricated for the task ahead, Todd had unzipped. I felt a warm splash on my back and head as he released the built-up beer that he'd obviously been guzzling while awaiting my arrival. I slurped as best I could as the wet stain spread across the tiles like a seasonal flood in Deniliquin.

I had been doing my best imitation of a sponge for about 15 minutes when there was a loud thump and I heard Scott's angry voice from the apartment below: "Are you fuckin' pissing again, Todd, cause it's dripping down my light fittings and short circuited the TV. Will you cut it out!"

Ungraciously, Todd screamed back before fetching a glass from the kitchen and, flopping his flaccid knob, began to dribble what little piss he had retained into it. "Here," he said and belched. "I like to see fine things desecrated. It turns me on."

Just then Todd's flat mate arrived home and shrieked "That's our best fucking crystal!" as he grabbed the glass to tip its contents down the sink. The gurgling drain more or less paralleled the sounds my stomach was attempting to suppress.

"What do you want for dinner?" Todd's flat mate asked when he'd scrubbed the glass to such pristine cleanliness it would have done an obsessive compulsive proud. A grunt from Todd somehow translated into a preference for lentil curry and peas. And a desire to watch *Sixty Minutes* because they'd advertised this really rather gripping debate on the parlous state of the economy.

Now, I'm as interested as the next slave in how sales tax will affect the price of my next sling or whether the import duty on Crisco will force me to a cheaper brand, but not when I'm being dragged through puddles of stale piss with a tongue coated with last week's mold while being swatted on the back with a crop, and a ten-inch butt plug protruding from my well-beaten ass yelling "Yes sir! No sir! Three bags full sir!"

Todd's flat mate complained that he couldn't hear the TV for all our grunting and verbal sparring and turned the volume up. This led Scott downstairs to prod his ceiling with a vigor that suggested this was not an uncommon occurrence. He was obviously releasing a lot of pent up frustration.

"Chow's ready," Todd's flat mate said after the microwave pinged, Suddenly the two of them sat down to a thawed and zapped lentil curry with a ready-made supermarket salad, and chapattis. My meal was under the table: Todd's red and very swollen dick. "I've been using the Accu-Jack," he'd admitted earlier. Prodding it with my tongue was like rimming a sponge cake; all I really felt like doing was sticking a candle in it and singing *Happy Birthday*.

As I was working the swollen appendage in my mouth, Todd moved uncomfortably on the chair and the long liquid *phhht* of a lethal fart assaulted my nostrils. Without so much as a "pardon me" he continued to shovel the curry into his mouth, again shifting in his seat.

I abhor bad manners. Enough is enough even for the best behaved slave and I was brimful of it. I stood up suddenly and my limp, very dissatisfied cock brushed the edge of the table.

"Hey, get your dick out of the lettuce," Todd's flat mate yelled.

Mustering my discarded jeans and a little pride, I marched out, slamming the door behind me. The commotion brought Scott to his door, itching for another verbal onslaught, but he just gaped as I nakedly descended the stairs.

By way of explanation as I passed, I said, "I pissed in their salad." And kept walking.

# THE BEAR'S GUIDE TO DEPILATORY WAX

The wind was icy around my ears, but it scarcely registered. I had come this far and I so wanted to take that one step more that would finally wipe away the years of pain. I had endured for twenty long years, surely that was enough. I knew from experience that God was a cruel bastard, I'd never realized until now He was also a sadist.

A lifetime of pain and misery versus sweet oblivion. It was a no-brainer, and yet I hesitated. I was chicken shit. All those people who'd called me names, who'd bullied and belittled me, were right. I couldn't let them be. That would be the ultimate humiliation. As the only person who ever really loved me, I wrapped my arms around my body in final surrender.

One last glance at the dark swirling waters below. It looked so inviting, so warm from my position atop the railing meant to prevent pedestrians from plummeting over the side of the bridge. Ah, sweet serenity. I silently cursed the world. I jumped.

"Ewww, he's an ugly little bastard," are the first words I remember hearing as a child. My parents assured me they weren't the first but all comments, said within my hearing, were of a similar ilk. The one I remember was uttered by my Uncle Joe when I was around four. My aunt Connie reprimanded primly, "Joe. Manners." Then peering at me through her spectacles added, "But the little tyke is on the homely side."

I discovered years later that I'd got my revenge in advance by pissing on Connie's nice new frock when she picked me up out of my crib as a baby and let out an exclamation of surprise similar to her husband's. I wish I could remember that. It seems she'd commented on the excess of hair on my portly little body by describing me as a 'monkey baby.'

The same night as my uncle's outburst I lay awake listening to my mum sob in her bedroom next door. She and dad were discussing me loudly enough that I could hear just about every word. They seemed to be of the belief that with ugliness came deafness. It would have been a godsend.

"Perhaps we should check with the hospital. They might have given us the wrong baby," she said. I insulted her self-esteem because both my dad and mum were singularly attractive – everyone said so – and were expected to produce a brood of remarkable-looking offspring. Like my older sister, for example, or my younger brother. Both excellent examples of superior genetics.

My mother, for example, was the top-rated weather girl, as well as moonlighting as the impeccably groomed wallpaper who turned the letters around on a popular quiz program. My dad, was a local political figure of whom great things were expected. They pushed family values and old-fashioned mum and dad apple-pie virtues in my dad's poll-time literature, littered with family photos. Just not mine. I was never part of that family.

The family I was part of was the gaggle of relatives that met for Christmas and occasions such as birthdays, deaths, and anniversaries. I hardened myself over the years after overhearing people say, "It would have been a blessing if he'd died at birth." Or "It's a punishment from God because the parents are so handsome and so successful."

My mum was big on the God angle. I was standing next to her clutching her fashionable designer jeans when the hospital rang her with the news that I was not the 'wrong' child. She sighed stalwartly, patted me on the head, and said with a resignation that will live with me forever, "I guess, sweetheart, you're our cross that God meant us to bear."

The family trotted off to church every Sunday morning where I prayed with all the fervor my little heart could muster for God to make me if not handsome, then not totally butt ugly. I screwed my eyes up real tight and whispered my prayer to the heavens at church each week, as well as every night before bed. In the morning, after I woke up, I would run to the bathroom to see what changes God had made. I was always keen to see the difference as I knew He was working on it because each morning I'd wake up and there'd be a smattering of dead hairs among the sheets, obviously ones that God had pulled out during the night.

I realized He had a lot on his plate, but He really needed to concentrate a bit harder on what He was doing for me. So I slipped in an extra prayer during lunch break at school. I'd lock myself in one of the toilet cubicles and pray for all I was worth. It made little difference. I did wonder whether God felt insulted because I'd prayed while I was in a toilet. Maybe it was just bad manners on my part.

There's just so much disappointment a young kid can endure before he spits the dummy. After three months of my promises to devote my life to God if He would take away my affliction, plus assurances from my parents and the minister that God definitely listened to everyone's prayers – although they always tagged it with the addendum, 'but God doesn't always answer the way you expect, but he will answer' – I looked in the mirror for the last time in my childhood. Not only had God not answered my prayers, the hairs in my bed that I'd taken as a sign He cared were merely natural attrition as I rubbed them off my body moving about in the bed during my sleep.

In fact, I was sprouting hair faster than I was shedding it. I covered my mirror with one of my mum's shawls and I never looked in it again, learning to brush my hair by just combing it back away from my face. I never looked in the bathroom mirror, always keeping my eyes lowered, avoided shop windows by looking straight ahead, and never saw the look of disgust or horror in people's eyes by concentrating on a spot on their forehead. I became inured to teasing and bullying in school and managed, all things considered, to have a comparatively happy childhood, albeit without any close friends.

I thought everything was going to be all right.

Then, pow, came high school. And puberty. With it came more hair, now on parts of my body that hadn't seen it before: my armpits, my face, and my groin. Suddenly, I developed pimples, a croaky voice, and became a podgy little piggy. I also developed a devoted crush on one of the school prefects. Male.

After dinner one night, as I waddled off to my bedroom to do my homework, I heard my mother sigh. "Just when we thought he couldn't get any worse."

If my parents thought they had a cross to bear, it was purely cosmetic, because now that I was forced to play sport once a week and endure phys ed classes, both of which meant stripping naked to shower in front of my tormentors, my life was a living hell. The looks of disbelief at my hairy body, especially my back, soon turned to derision. Name calling quickly followed: Monkey Boy, Neanderthal Man, as well as the generic terms of abuse, butt ugly, fugly. Etc. I'd heard them all my life. Even my younger brother and elder sister joined in the baiting, only from the security of the school yard, however. They were remarkably friendly and non-judgmental at home, but put them among their peers and they were the first to throw verbal stones.

When I could, I avoided sports or phys ed, feigning sickness or injury, skipping school, anything at all to escape the humiliation. My one solace was my love of all scholastic pursuits. Not all of them; I tended toward the more artistic, the more scientific the basis the less interested I became. Not for me physics, chemistry, mathematics, I reveled in literature, art, film, and, particularly, graphic novels, especially those with hyper-masculine heroes and superheroes, particularly if they wore tight trousers or cock hugging tights. Even though the artists never drew anything as exciting as a bulge, my imagination colored in what was behind that fabric.

I'd begun experimenting with my dick as soon as I learned about masturbation. It was pleasurable, no doubt about that, and I could fill my head with all sorts of taboo sexuality with any man I could conjure. Eventually, fantasy wears thin and I ached to share my secret pastime with someone else. A special friend. Or two.

Talk in the change rooms after sport among the alpha males often revolved around their open boasting about circle jerks, some of the older boys telling of girls from the local high school who were expert at blow jobs. I knew what these things meant because I'd found videos of them on the net. I ran them over and over while I jerked my cock, spewing the results of my activity into tissues – I kept a box in my bedroom for just such occasions – that way I could flush them so I wouldn't be caught. Unlike Lionel Hill who did it in his socks until his mother twigged to why they were a little on the stiff side and reeked of…I advised Lionel that a box of tissues cost less than two dollars at the local supermarket. Instead of thanking me, he shoved me to the ground and called me 'faggot.'

That was the last time I attempted to help anyone.

I made a few friends at high school, other misfits and outcasts who didn't flinch at my sprouting body hair or that I had five o'clock shadow at around half past one. Some of us fumbled our way through drunken experimentation although I seemed to be the only one predisposed to experimenting with the same gender. Slowly and painfully, I learned the intricacies of intimacy and falling in adolescent love. The objects of my affection were always the boys who most tormented me. I was a glutton for punishment.

There was nothing remotely effeminate about me, the hair alone putting paid to that. I looked more akin to a young wharf laborer than a fairy. None the less, 'faggot' was the favorite put-down other schoolmates flung at me. If they were spiteful at school they were downright malicious on the net. Social media gave them the cover of anonymity, and they did not hold back on their name-calling and their bullying. It got so bad that I logged onto the net only to research homework and to watch porn.

I blocked all senders on my email account except those essential to my schoolwork, and my very closest friends, sending the remainder to the spam dump where they obviously belonged. It was galling that I was also wary of emails from my own brother and sister. They were the pride of my parents who used their boasting rights at every opportunity to espouse their children's superiority. Not mine, however. Regardless of how hard I worked, or how great my achievement, it was often overlooked or else disregarded in the rush to compliment my siblings, no matter their scholastic record was lesser than my own.

It would have been easy to give in and just slack my way through high school, but I had visions of making a future for myself as far away from small city life as possible. By my reckoning – and remember, mathematics was never my forte – the larger the city, the more likelihood of a larger proportion of the 'differently beautied.' That was my little joke at the burgeoning politically correct rebranding of anything that was not mainstream.

If my calculations were correct, I would be able to hide my hideousness in a larger tertiary institution and secrete myself unobtrusively in a city large enough that ugly did not command the extraordinary attention that mine did in my home city. I was pathetic. My dreams were not of wealth, fame, opportunity or any of the myriad positives on offer to my more beautiful but less educated brother and sister. My dreams were not of the positive kind, they were more along the lines of the less negative.

Every penny I could do without from the meager allowance my parents gave me, or from the jobs that I took during my holidays, mail dropping brochures for the local supermarket, or flipping burgers for a fast food outlet that thought I was better in the kitchen than serving behind the counter – 'We don't want to put the customers off their food now, do we?' the manager said in justification – was saved for my escape.

My parents often discussed my future as my high school years drew to a close. Those times they didn't discuss it with me face-to-face, I'd overheard them talking to my sister who attended the local college. Her grades had been insufficient for her to attend a major university. Besides, her ambition was to marry a successful lawyer or IT entrepreneur.

"Please, dad, Esben can't go to the same college as me. I would be so humiliated," Susan moaned one night at a round-table family discussion. Family minus one: me. "I'd lose all my friends. I'd be an outcast."

Welcome to the club.

My mum commiserated, "We know, sweetheart. We want what's best for you, as well. We earmarked most of the future education funds we saved for you and your brother Tad. But we can't be seen playing favorites, we have to help Esben as well."

"Why?" Susan sneered. "It won't do him any good. He'll always be ugly."

"That's enough," my father said. My heart skipped a beat. My father was defending me? "With luck, Esben will choose one of those liberal arts universities that I've been steering him towards. He'll apply for a scholarship because I've been telling him the family finances are stretched to the limit and our support only goes so far, and the money we've put aside can go to your education—"

"Oh, daddy," Susan was almost flirting. "Why not put it toward something important, like my wedding?"

"We'll think about it, sweetheart."

"We're just waiting for Esben to make up his mind which end of the country he wants to go to," my mum added, to laughter all round.

When dad said he'd think about something that Susan suggested, it was in the bag.

I'm not one of those kids that think parents should subsidize their lives, but I did object to the willful manipulation of my future for the benefit of my brother and sister. I was angry. I'd come home with yet another superlative test score, hoping to receive a pat on the back or a throwaway 'well done,' but what I'd overheard through the closed kitchen door made my sense of fair play boil.

I stormed off to my bedroom, upended my desk drawer until I found what I was after, flicked through until I found the page, then took a number of deep breaths to regain my equilibrium and headed back to the kitchen, my heart steeled.

Slamming the front door to make it sound as if I'd just arrived home, I yelled, "Mum, dad, I've made a decision." I feigned excitement as I burst into the kitchen. My sister looked down her nose at me, while I pecked mum on the cheek, then stood in front of them all, bouncing on the balls of my feet to simulate my pleasure.

"What have you decided, son?" my dad asked.

"Where I want to go to university," I beamed, hiding the application behind my back.

Three faces suddenly turned their most hypocritical attention to me. I dragged a chair out, deliberately to annoy my mum who hates that, and sat watching their expectant faces. Oh, this was so choice.

"After that discussion we had a few months back, dad, about the economy and how it had affected the future education fund you'd set up for the three of us. Well, I did a bit of thinking about how selfish I was, expecting you to help out. Besides, I did a few calculations and it was going to take a lot of money to live on campus, pay rent, support myself, buy books and all that…"

I saw my dad go to object.

"Yes, I can apply for a scholarship, but even that won't pay all the bills. I'd likely have to get a job which would eat into study time. But, you know, there was a simple solution staring me in the face all the time."

I saw my enthusiasm was infectious but the others around the table were impatient for me to get to the point.

Ready, aim…

"I know I was being too ambitious with some of my choices, so I asked around about more local institutions. Like the community college where Susan goes."

The look of horror on my sister's face said it all. It was hard not to laugh.

"Okay," I continued, "it's not the ideal institution I had in mind, but it will give me some sort of certificate to flash at prospective employers, especially in this town. Plus, I get to stay at home. Oh, I'll pay rent, the same amount as Susan, and Tad when he gets older." I knew Susan paid zero, zilch, nada, for her accommodation and meals at home, although the family pretended otherwise.

"Besides, it will be great to have a big sis on the same campus. It will give us a chance to get to know each other better, hang out together, that sort of thing."

Susan groaned. "Kill me now."

I flashed the community college handbook at them, open at the application page. "I've chosen a course that is roughly the sort of thing I want to study. Look, I know it's not ideal, but I want you and dad to know I appreciate all you've done for me, and, well, I want to pull my weight, too, now that things are tight. I'll be able to live at home and help you out mum, and pay toward my keep instead of letting the bedroom lay idle."

Mum had no intention of allowing the room to remain a relic of my past, preserved in aspic. I'd heard her more than once discussing her plans for turning it into an office once I'd left the nest. I would be relegated to the couch upon my return visits, in expectation I wouldn't stay around long.

"I'm going right upstairs now to fill in the application."

I ignored the open-mouthed surprise on the three seated around the table and almost skipped out the door.

I wouldn't even have been out of earshot before Susan cried, "No, daddy, you can't let him. You promised he'd go far away."

Bullseye!

"Perhaps you overplayed the tight fiscal situation, dear," my mum chided.

"I could always promise to find the money to help him out if he leaves town, then once he's established I can claim the worsening financial situation means I have to renege on my offer," my dad said.

"Don't you dare give him one cent of my money," Susan demanded.

I'd heard enough. I had no intention of attending the local college. My future lay as far away from this city as I could go. I already knew the university and the course I wanted to take. I would bleed for it before I'd admit defeat.

It didn't take long before dad came to my bedroom. I was studiously engrossed in filling out the application form, by hand, rather than on the computer which would have been easier. This was for show, not for real.

"Son," dad said as he came into the bedroom.

"Oh, hi dad, I'm just getting my application ready. I'll drop it in tomorrow on the way to school."

"About that," he said, trying to take the sheet from me. I wasn't about to let it go. "Your mother and I have discussed matters and we feel that by tightening our belts here at home, getting Susan to contribute more…she's willing to do that in order for you to get the education you need."

Oh, brother. As if.

"Ah, dad, that's so sweet of her, and you and mum, but I would never expect a bigger share than what you gave Susan or what you have lined up for Tad."

Dad winced. I hope it hurt.

"I'll go and see the accountant tomorrow. Perhaps the financial situation is not as dire as we thought. Things are starting to pick up. We may be able to promise a little extra to help you out without sacrificing Susan and Tad's shares."

"It's okay, dad. I've made up my mind. Besides," I had to tread carefully, "a promise is really not all that helpful. Situations change, the money could dry up with another financial crisis and then where would I be? Half-way through my course work and no financial support. Unless I had a guaranteed income for at least the first two years, it would probably make it impossible for me. I could get a part-time job and save for the remaining years. So, thanks, dad, but the best solution is the local college. Besides, it will be good to have Susan to talk to. Better because I'll get to see you and mum every night of the week. If I went away, who knows, you might only see me once a year at Christmas."

I thought I saw dad's eyes light up at that deliberate provocation. Nah, they wouldn't even see me once a year.

The worst outcome of my plot was that I'd be no worse off than I already was. I had enough money put aside that I wouldn't go without my first year, but I would have to be frugal, and I would have to get a part-time job. The best outcome would be to wrest a little cash out of dad to supplement my living expenses.

I heard mum and dad discussing my plans throughout the evening, voices raised in anger when Susan joined in. Later she came to my bedroom while I worked on my real application. Seething with hostility, she spat, "Don't for a minute think I'll have anything at all to do with your sorry ass if you come to my college. I'll cut you dead. No one will ever know we're related."

I turned to her, smiling sweetly. "Oh, don't worry, Susan. I intend following you around the campus making your life a pure hell, just like you have me all these years. I'll make sure that everyone knows Neanderthal Man is your blood brother, not the adopted kid you've always maintained. I'll try out for the swim team and I'll dedicate every win to my supportive sister, Susan, as I stand there in my Speedos, holding my trophy aloft, my hairy body visible to all your friends. Every time I do something that attracts attention, in all modesty, I'll say "I couldn't have done it without the love and support of my family, especially my adorable sister, Susan."

"You wouldn't dare."

"I'm already setting up my Facebook page which is a tribute to my darling sister who convinced me to attend the same college as her because she couldn't live without my brotherly love and friendship."

I clicked the computer screen over to the page I had tentatively set up and which included a grotesque photoshopped pic of me and Susan sharing an ice cream.

Her in her bikini at the beach, me with my head superimposed professionally on the body of a film werewolf wearing swimming trunks.

"Oh my God," she screamed, before fleeing the room. "Mu-um. Da-ad."

Over the next few days I chanced upon numerous family discussion to which I had not been invited. Still, I displayed the same happy enthusiasm for the local college as I had at the outset, while planning what I needed from my bedroom to make my life comfortable on the other side of the country. I knew I would never be back and, even if I were, every trace of my existence would have been obliterated.

In the end, the stress got to my family. My dad capitulated, offering me a lucrative cash incentive to 'choose the best course available' and not to restrict my sights to a small city like the one in which we lived. It could not have been more obvious that I was unloved and unwanted – a family embarrassment, like an uncle no one wants to talk about.

My parents made it evident that my welcome, should I bother to return, would be less than fulsome. Dad paid for my plane fare, one-way, saying I should contact him if I was returning so he could get the cheapest rate. He dropped me at the airport, none of the others bothered to say au revoir, treating it like it was just another day. For them it was, for me it was the beginning of the rest of my life.

In fact, it was the same old/same old. Dad shook my hand at the airport, wished me the best of luck, and was gone. At the other end I was met with cold indifference by university authorities, lecturers, class mates, right down to, and including, the on-campus GLTBIQ group which prided itself on being all inclusive. You were accepted if you were gay, lesbian, transgender, bi, intersex, or merely identified as queer. Unless you were ugly and hairy.

That first year I managed to hook up with a few closeted guys or a few out and proud men. I was never sure if I was a pity fuck or they were just so drunk they didn't care. All I knew was that it was sex without affection. I longed for the kissing, the cuddling, and the touching. What I got was the fucking, the sucking, and the blowing. There was never a date involved. They may have wanted me briefly for sex, but they sure didn't want to be seen with me in public.

The first few months away from 'home' I tested the waters, sending a number of cheery emails to each and every member of the family about my progress, my activities, everything but the personal. No one bothered to reply. I rang and left messages on the home line as well as my parents' cell phones. Nothing. No one could say I didn't try.

My reaction was relief more than sadness, although I did envy other people their close relationship with their family. My lack was yet another nail in the coffin that was my unattractiveness. I didn't exactly loathe myself, I loathed the outer shell. Inside, I was resilient and bounced back easily from the dark depressions that sometimes gripped me, especially after a drunken coupling.

At least, I bounced back each time until I met Alan. He was gorgeous and I'm afraid I developed a puppy dog crush on him. He encouraged it because he loved being adored and no one loved him more than I did. I knew he was arrogant and cared for no one but himself but who can stop their heart once it's set on someone? I certainly couldn't. It was my first real time with those wonderful feelings in my stomach.

I was so starry-eyed I followed him around campus, ingratiating myself into his twink group. They were all gay. A group of spoiled rich kids who had money, power, and their own self-importance as the glue that bound them together. What I had in common was my desire to bed Alan. The others in the group also had that dream; those that hadn't already achieved that end. They also had their intense dislike of me in common. They began by calling me Frankentwink to my face, believing they were so much cleverer than the folk back 'home' who coined the equally trite 'Neanderthal Man.' I use the word 'home' merely as descriptive of where I grew up, with no feeling at all of belonging. In that sense I was close enough to being a stateless person.

My infatuation with Alan probably would have run its course in time; the subject of my adoration had no intention of inviting me to his bed. I overheard him once tell his best friend that the reason he kept me around was that my ugliness enhanced his beauty when people saw us side by side. I was disappointed, sure, but also elated because it meant he would keep me around.

However, my affection for Alan was short-circuited one night at a party to which I was invited. These events normally saw me fetching and carrying for Alan and his mates, the eternal butt of jokes. They were painful affairs sometimes when I watched my beloved flirting with other partygoers, sometimes fucking in a dark corner where he knew one of his mates would ensure I saw him. My distress was their entertainment. I had such low self-esteem at that stage, I didn't care. My dream of a new life in a new city had proven as hollow as my prayers to a non-existent God.

The fateful night, Alan and his gang were patently bored with the party, the choice of music, the alcohol, the party drugs, and the other guests whom they believed were so far below them as to not even warrant their attention. It was too late to head elsewhere so they made the best of a bad lot but swilling alcohol like it was bottled water. Ennui and privilege often lead young men astray. They turned their boredom against me, the most vulnerable person in the house. They encouraged me to drink because tonight was the night Alan was going to 'invite me home.' I wanted so much to believe it that I drank their celebratory beverages, never suspecting they had doctored them.

There was a lot of good-natured teasing and for the first time in my life I began to feel like I belonged. Poor fool me.

"Alan thinks you're so sexy. He'd love to see you strip. Do a little dance for him, Esben," one of his friends encouraged.

I would do anything for Alan and if he wanted a strip, a strip he would have. Someone hushed everyone, while a CD was inserted and the sounds of bump and grind filled the room. I threw everything I had into my drunken performance, my mind visualizing myself as the sexiest thing to ever shed his clothes. Love poured out of me as I slithered and squirmed although my best moves were met with raucous laughter and now that I think back on it, I tripped and tumbled more than slithered.

I was oblivious to how stupid I must have appeared. When I finally removed the last stitch of my clothes, there were enough gross-out comments they sobered me quickly. I'd been conned. I grabbed my clothes but they were roughly yanked from my grasp.

"Why don't we give out ugly little fur bear here a Brazilian?" Alan suggested. A cheer went up and a number of partygoers went off in search of shaving gear, to return with a razor, depilatory strips, and a dusty old kit of depilatory wax they'd found shoved at the back of a bathroom cabinet.

I struggled but there were too many of them holding me down. Alan began by attempting to shave my shoulders but the blade clogged so often that he made no headway. Next he tried the strips even as I kicked and screamed as he tore hairs from my back. I cursed the partygoers, I cursed my parents, I cursed life in general that no one came to my aid.

The wax was the final indignity. Someone remembered how to melt it, another how to spread it on an area with the wooden spatula. They chose a spot on my ass, liberally applying the hot wax, waiting for it to cool before the party began the countdown. 10...9...8...7...

The pain was incredible. While one part of my brain admired women for going through such torture, another registered the agony of my body. I felt violated in the worst sense. Someone gasped, "Look, he's bleeding. I think you pulled skin off." The hands that had held me so firmly suddenly let me free.

Through my tears I could see the looks of horror on some men's faces, while others were too drunk to understand and continued to cackle like broody hens. I staggered to my feet, grabbing my clothes, and headed to the bathroom, locking myself inside. I was a mess. My tears stained my drunken face, my back a patchwork of failed depilatory, my ass skinned and bleeding. The amount of blood had scared them but once I cleaned the wounds it wasn't as bad as it looked at first. As I was treating the wound, Alan came to the door begging for admittance. My heart sank. I knew if he apologized, I'd be right back where I started. I knew I would go home with him and everything would continue as before.

Being a weak bastard, I let him in. I was unprepared, however, for the violence that followed. He grabbed me by the neck, shoving me against the wall, his sour breath in my face.

"Don't even think about reporting this you fugly little troll. Unless you want to be thrown out on that hairy ass of yours. Everyone at the party will swear you got drunk and begged to be shaved. No one will support you. So you lost a bit of skin. Big deal."

He never bothered to look at the wound to see how little skin I'd actually lost. Obviously, he believed I'd been injured more than I had.

"I can destroy you and don't doubt for a minute that I will if you make it necessary."

I couldn't believe my Alan was treating me like this. There was no concern for me, just for his reputation. I couldn't control my emotions. I began sobbing at the betrayal and I couldn't stop. That pulled him up a little and his tirade ceased. He fumbled in his pocket and pulled out a handful of notes. "Here," he said, shoving them in my pocket. "Get a taxi, go to hospital and have it checked out if it's that bad. They'll patch you up. Never come near us again or so help me…"

He spat in my face, turned on his heels and slammed out of the bathroom. I slid down the wall and sat on the floor until the wave of emotion subsided. Gingerly, I then dressed and slipped out of the house to a chorus of snickers and drunken jeers. No one came to my aid. I stumbled back onto the street and made my way to nearest major intersection. There was no way I wanted to hang about the party waiting for a passing cab.

I hadn't long to wait although the first two must have thought I looked as bad as I felt for when I hailed them, they quickly switched off their vacant lights. The third driver was not as fussy. I gave my dorm address, settling into the back seat, where I began to appraise my life. Yeah, I felt sorry for myself. I knew things were not about to change. I also knew there were people out there much less fortunate than me who managed to get through life with a modicum of happiness and satisfaction. But they weren't me. I'd copped it all my life and tonight was the proverbial straw.

My despair was a bottomless black pit and I no longer had the strength to stop myself falling in. I changed my drop-off address, steeling my determination. The closer we got, the more adamant was I that it was the only solution to my pain.

I wasn't foolish enough to have the taxi drop me right near the bridge, so I walked the two blocks, my tears totally self-indulgent now. There's nothing worse than wallowing in self-pity and my thoughts that everyone would be sorry at my demise were so far off the mark it's a wonder I didn't laugh out loud. Almost mechanically, I climbed the railing, perched there for a few seconds – and jumped.

Chicken shit. I panicked at the last and grabbed for the railing catching it just before my downward plummet. I wrenched my shoulder and yelled in pain. Cursing, because I couldn't even kill myself right, I pulled myself back over the railing, falling heavily on the pavement skinning my arms. What a sorry sight I was.

Needing more courage in my endeavors, I saw the lights from a pub nearby and staggered in their direction, still determined to go through with my final solution. I was so oblivious to my surroundings that my self-harm almost became a moot point when a car came close to obliterating me as I crossed the busy road. I could have just lain down and waited, but the idea of the impact of a fast-moving vehicle against my body – no appeal there.

At least the pub was warm when I pushed my way inside, making for the bar. It was a moderately busy night although a quick glance around revealed all the patrons were men, most of them older men with facial hair, and the sort of masculine beefy bodies I associated with truckers and manual workers. Just the place to get my head kicked in. Ignoring them, I found a stool to perch on, making myself as small a target as possible because I'd already noticed a number of groups staring at me.

Before I could attract the barman's attention another bloke, dressed in jeans and a plaid shirt open at the neck to display a spout of thick hair, pushed in beside me.

"Buy you a drink, mate?" he asked.

I knew he didn't mean me, so I didn't react. He nudged me with his shoulder. "Hey, you asleep?"

I looked up then into the face of one of the most gorgeous men I'd ever seen. He must have been around forty, with a trim goatee and moustache. He was bulky in the body, but trim with it. He was smiling at me.

"You mean me?" I stuttered.

"Who else?"

"Um…no one's ever bought me a drink before," I replied.

"More fool them," he chuckled.

"Why would you buy me a drink?"

"You look as if you could do with the company," he said. His eyes bored into me as if he could see every secret of my miserable existence.

I plucked up the courage to ask, "No…no other reason?"

"Well, I don't normally start off a conversation like this, but I'd really like to take you home and have me and the boyfriend bugger the ass off you."

"You're gay?"

"The whole bar is sweetheart. Gay or gay curious."

"You don't look it."

"Not sure that's much of a compliment these days. He called the barman, "Sam, over here, mate." Then he turned to me, "What are you having?"

It took two drinks to warm to Kevin who kept rubbing his crotch against my leg to let me know he had a hard on with my name on it.

"Why would you want to have sex with me?" I asked. "When someone as good looking as you could have any man in the bar."

"Take a look around," he smiled. "You see anyone else in here half as good-looking as you?"

"Just about everyone," I said truthfully.

He laughed uproariously.

"Hey, Sam. Come and settle an argument for me."

"What is it?"

"Esben. Sam."

I nodded to the barman who looked as if he could crush me just by flexing his bicep.

"Esben here wants to know why I'm trying to get into his pants. Take a look around and tell us who the cutest thing in the bar is."

Sam did as instructed, then returned his gaze to me, nodding. "Sweetcheeks here is just about the cutest cub we had in here since I don't know when," Sam said.

"Cub," I said.

Kevin explained. "This is a bear bar."

I must have looked puzzled because Kevin went on. "You know, hairy men or men who like hairy men. Bears."

I was flabbergasted. "There are men who like hairy men?"

"Hmm, new to this, are you?"

"You don't think I'm ugly?"

Kevin looked at me strangely. "You been knocked about bad, kid?"

I couldn't help it, the dam burst. My whole sad life poured out of me like a tsunami of despair. Kevin didn't interrupt, and Sam kept supplying the drinks, while I unloaded all the stupid baggage I'd carried around for my twenty-odd years. Occasionally he hugged me when it all got too much and the tears scalded my face. He just held me until I could continue with my story.

Somewhere during my tale, which seemed as long as *War and Peace*, we left the bar and I found myself shuddering as we drove over the bridge from which I was determined to jump a few hours earlier. I'd completed the story up to the evening's events by the time we pulled into Kevin's apartment building car park. I was washed out, ready to collapse, so Kevin held me up as we caught the elevator to his floor.

Inside his apartment, he steered me to the bedroom where he undressed me as I lay passively on the bed. He admired my body, complimenting me at every turn on my beauty, my muscles, my ass. He even leaned in to kiss the spot where they'd torn my skin.

"Bastards," Kevin spat.

As I snuggled into his warm king-size bed, he stripped off his clothes so I could admire his body. He was as hairy as me, the fur covering almost every square inch. I had been taught it was ugly, but on Kevin…well, it made me hard. He slipped into bed beside me, spooning me. I felt his hairy chest and belly rub against my back.

"You tired, Baby Bear?"

I couldn't stifle the yawn and before I knew it, I was asleep in his arms, more secure than I had ever been. I didn't wake until I felt the bed in front of me sink as another body joined us. His arms went around me. He obviously hadn't expected a foreign body because his hand explored me until he turned on the bedside lamp. My eyes were wide open in expectation of trouble. The newcomer leaned up on his arm surveying me.

"What do we have here?" he said, although he didn't sound particularly annoyed.

The guy was bigger than Sam the bartender with muscles to match. I looked at his biceps and almost drooled.

He saw me. "You like, eh?" He flexed. "Go on, you can touch."

I reached out and squeezed his arms. They were solid as granite.

He lay back down, pulling me closer to him so we were chest pelt to chest pelt. "You're a cute little fucker," he said. "Do you mind if I kiss you?"

He held me under the chin. It was all I could do to croak, "Please."

I could have died in a kiss like that. His tongue pushed between my lips and I opened up to let him in. His mouth covered mine and he poked, prodded and sucked as I welcomed the most wonderful feeling of my life. He obviously liked it as much as I did because his hard cock poked into my stomach. Tentatively, I reached down to wrap my hand around it. I had never felt anything so big and thick.

I had to push him off because I was in danger of suffocating, his kiss was so intense.

"How about you suck me, Baby Bear? Would you like that?"

"Yes, sir."

Disengaging from the sleeping Kevin's arms, I kneeled between the Daddy Bear's thighs and began work on his balls. He lay back watching me in action. "That feels so good. Lick those balls, cub. Make Daddy Bear glad to meet you." I concentrated so hard on pleasing this mammoth of a man that it wasn't until I felt my ass cheeks pulled apart that I realized Kevin had woken up.

"Manny, this is Esben."

"Hello, Esben. Glad you could join our family tonight."

I didn't stop trying to get his cock into my mouth to speak. I looked up at him and nodded. He could see how pleased I was. I gasped when Kevin's tongue found my puckered hole and pushed into me. Everyone else I'd fucked with had found my hairy ass a total turn off unless they were pissed to the gills, but Kevin hummed as if mine was the choicest ass in the world.

"Oh, daddy, wait until you see his cute little hairy cub ass. It will send you berserk," Kevin said leaning over me to kiss his lover.

I'd never been involved in a three-way before, I'd had enough difficulty just attracting one partner.

"Open him up for me," Manny said. "I gotta get me a piece of that ass when you've finished with him."

Kevin got off the bed, returning moments later. I knew why when I felt a cold gel squeezed against my butthole and then Kevin began to push two fingers slowly inside me.

"God, you're tight," he whispered. I tried unsuccessfully to take Manny totally in my mouth. It was just impossible so I contented myself with sucking his knob and the first few inches of his shaft while jacking the base. I'd almost forgotten Kevin until I felt something blunt at my sphincter after he'd removed his fingers.

I tensed for a moment until Manny drew my attention back to his prick. Still, I was unprepared for the bear-sized cock that breached my ass even though Kevin took his time. It stung like buggery but there was no way I was ever gonna back out now. Kevin remained still until I got used to him and then I pushed my ass against his cock to show him I was ready for more. We kept at it until he sank the entire length inside me.

"How's that, Esben?" he whispered.

"That feels great. Go ahead, fuck me."

I'd never wanted to be possessed as much as I wanted these two men to possess me.

Manny held me as his lover pounded my ass, spurred on by my demands to fuck me harder. Kev obliged in spades. I flexed my ass muscles as he plunged in and out, wishing it would never end. But with the curse of a thousand demons, Kevin spattered my insides with his spunk as Manny encouraged us both with the foulest dream scenarios I'd ever heard.

When Kevin pulled out, I felt cum dribble from my ass. "Hold it in Baby Bear, you'll need all the lubrication you can get," he advised.

"I don't want to hurt you, Esben, but I'd really love to plow that cute young Baby Bear ass," Manny confirmed.

"I want you to fuck me, Daddy Bear."

I lay on my back, retracting my knees to my chest. Manny looked at me and I saw the lust in his eyes. Kevin scooted over to rub lubrication on his lover's thick cock and to add a little more to my already expanded hole. I watched Manny's face as he pushed his cock head against my hole. I was prepared for the worst but the head slipped in easily. He pushed slowly but forcefully, expanding my elastic sphincter, filling me until I was fit to burst. I groaned as the friction stung a little but I didn't want him to stop.

Once he was all the way in, he stopped to allow me to get accustomed to his huge prick. I whispered the magic words and he slowly withdrew to plunge back in again. He was touching places that had never felt a cock before, forcing my own dick to drool pre-cum.

He increased his pace as he saw I could take it until he was pounding me into the mattress. "You like that, Baby Bear? You like my thick Daddy Bear cock buried up your ass?"

"I love it," I whimpered.

Kevin didn't want to miss out on the action and squeezed between us, engulfing my cock in his mouth.

"Oh, shit," I panted. "I won't be able to hold off if you keep doing that."

"Come for us," Manny said. "Give Kevin your spunk. Let me feel your ass spasm around my prick."

Kevin's mouth was like honey and I knew I was seconds away from blowing my load.

"Here it comes," I screamed. "Take it all. Swallow it."

Manny increased his pace, burying his cock in my guts, my clenching ass bringing him quickly to the boil so that I felt his jets of spunk deep inside me. He kept fucking long after Kevin had sucked every ounce of cum from my balls. Manny finally gave one last grunt, and kept his cock inside me, shuddering as he shot his last spurt. He huffed his satisfaction before slowly pulling his cock from my well-fucked hole.

I was sorry it was over because now I'd have to leave and I had been enjoying just lying with Kevin. I got out of bed to retrieve my clothes.

"What are you doing?" Kevin asked.

"I thought you'd want me to go now you've come," I said.

Manny pulled me back onto the bed. "You're not going anywhere, Baby Bear."

Kevin went to fetch a wet cloth to clean us all up, then we collapsed on the bed, me in the center, cuddled by two hairy men.

"You can't go," Kevin said. "You haven't fucked me yet."

"And I definitely want another go at your ass," Manny added. "In fact, there are so many things we want to do to you, Esben, we may never let you go."

## Lydian

## ABOUT THE AUTHOR

Barry Lowe writes about love and sex so he won't forget how to do it. When he's not scribbling his adventures for the Sydney gay weekly *SX¸* or out doing field research, he's writing about love's wonderful variations for a series of smut eBooks, novels and anthologies for Lydian Press.

Go to www.barrylowe.info

ANTHOLOGIES By Barry Lowe

BUSTING BILLY'S BUTT - eBook & Print

Four On The Floor
Jolly Rogering
The Devil His Due
Never Take Candy from Strangers
Done Like A Dinner
In The Family Way
Right Up His Alley
Group Therapy

THE MAJOR AND THE MINERS - eBook & Print

A Serpent in Paradise
Desperate Remedies
Joshua's Story
Emerald City
Danny's Revenge
Future Tense

ROMANCING THE BONE - eBook and Print

Carbon Dating
Let the Games Begin
Taking the Bait
Party Whip
Team Player
Davy Jones' Locker
Here's to You, Mr Robinson
Gay Dungeon for the Straight Boy
OMG! Santa's Got a Six-Pack
Vlad the Impaler
Meta-Analysis of the Effects of Love on Tofu

LIKE FATHER LIKE SON - eBook and Print

Man of the Hour
Like Father Like Son
Sonny & Shared
Sonny Side Up
Eclipse Of The Son
Son & Games
Where The Sun Don't Shine
The Sun Shines Out Of His Ass
Have Son Will Travel

COCK-EYED OPTIMISTS - eBook and Print

A Red Rose Before Crying
Too Frocked to Care
The Three Spooges
Love and the Odor of Red Leatherette
It's All Greek to Me
Hard On His Heels
Salted Mixed Sluts
The New Dad's Club

THE MORE THE MERRIER - eBook and Print

Marine Biology
Flesh for Fantasy
Buck's Night
Four On The Floor
Sluts & Satyrs
Framing the Picture of Dorian Gray
Fuck Buddy
Seven Card Studs
Dude, Where's The Bar?
New Year's Steve

THE BOY IS A BOTTOM - eBook and Print

    Marine Biology
    Marine Animals
    Attack of the Ass Bandits
    The Arab Downstairs
    Clockwork Derriere
    Creaming the Party Dip
    Top of the World
    Route 666: Signal Driver
    The Butler Did Him
    Fifty Shades of Fey
    Spinning the Bottom

ROUGH & READY -  eBook and Print

    Stocks & Shared
    Scarface
    Ceps: Mad about Muscle
    The Plumbers' Mate*
    Climbing Up the Wall
    Little Red Rides da Hood
    The Dex Factor

BABY, I'M NOT A MONSTER - eBook and Print

    The Vampire's Guide to Dental Hygiene
    Stupid Cupid
    Gadigal
    Pride & Joy
    Seeing Things
    My Dad's a Vampire
    Guys & Trolls
    Jailhouse Cock
    The Skinhead Upstairs

THE GRAVY TRAIN - eBook & Print

> In the Soup
> Salad Days
> Whores d'Oeuvres
> Beefed Up and Porked
> Torte A Lesson
> Café or Lay

YOUR BOYFRIEND IS HOT - eBook and Print

> From Here to Fraternity
> Stripping His Assets
> Indecent Exposure
> Middle Man for Madame Blavatsky
> A Cook's Tour
> Topping the Pizza Delivery Boy

OMG! NOT ANOTHER GAY EROTICA ANTHOLOGY?

> OMG! My Dad's a Stripper!
> OMG! The College Jock's a Nudist!
> OMG! Put Some Clothes On!
> OMG! My Uncle's a Fairy!
> OMG! Satan Wants a Blow Job!
> OMG! My Dad's Got Tits!
> OMG! Santa's Got a Six-pack!

For all Barry's titles please visit his page at:
lydianpress.com

*Lydian Press* is dedicated to bringing you the finest GLBTQ erotic literature on the web.

Visit us on the web at:

http://lydianpress.com

www.ingramcontent.com/pod-product-compliance
Lightning Source LLC
Chambersburg PA
CBHW051108050726
47592CB00002B/721